KEPT

© Theresa Jacobs 2017

All rights reserved. This book or any portion thereof may not be reproduced or used in any manner whatsoever without the express written permission of the publisher except for the use of brief quotations in a book review.

This book is dedicated, first and foremost, to my husband, Duane Minshull, who bears all the hours I spend working. To my dearest friends Aimie Pagendam, Leslie Grant, and Jacqueline Leahey who have to read, listen, and partake in this journey along with me, whether willingly or not. They're my peeps.

I'd like to thank Jason Berry for being a first-time beta reader, your insights are always welcome. And to the amazing author, Israel Finn, believe it or not, your last name somehow created Finnegan, and through him, this tale.

Thank you, Novel Nurse Editing, for all the hours and hard work. Anyone out there looking for a dedicated editor with strong work ethic, look no farther.
https://www.novelnurseediting.com/

R.L. Weeks of Dark Wish Design for the Cover, and the title tip.
https://www.facebook.com/groups/darkwishdesigns/

Table of Contents

1. Gaia
2. Changes
3. Earths Demise
4. Days Go By
5. Hope
6. Helen
7. Now What
8. The Men, The Women
9. Seven Sleeps
10. Hoopla
11. Are we there yet
12. The Expedition
13. A New Day
14. A New Life
15. A Life Lived

1. Gaia

Finnegan's mouth pulled up into a grin. He drew in a deep breath of icy air and took a step forward. He felt free. In fact, he couldn't recall the last time he felt this free. A high wind gusted through the pines, echoed off the white peaks, and reverberated down the mountainside. His thick-soled Baffin boots cracked the wafer-thin top layer of snow. It gave with a snap before his foot sunk past his ankles into the soft down below. He enjoyed the heft of his Remington 798 in his left hand, as he curled his fingers around the wood stock. His eyes traced the tree line in the distance, and he thought about what his prey would be today. Somewhere from a distance, he thought he heard his name called. He cocked his head and listened. The wind caressed his cheek with its biting frost. The white plateau before him displayed a picture-perfect postcard, an unmarred landscape of white, the deep green pine trees a backdrop. The voice came again, a soft whisper on the wind. Somewhere in his mind, Finnegan knew it was time to go, but he held the vista before him not yet ready to leave.

The land waved before his eyes, as a heatwave across hot asphalt, and the air swirled in a shimmer as it wisped away the scene before him.

He groaned low in his throat as his heart felt the weight of reality sink in. The dream floated away. He held his eyes closed, wanting the freedom of the dream to return. His only wish was to be back in the mountains hunting. To breathe in the fresh, cold air, knowing at the end of the day he'd be skinning dinner by a roaring fire.

Recalling where he currently was, his stomach clenched as imaginary vomit rose into his esophagus, and he fought the sensation.

"Finn?"

The soft voice drifted to his ears, and he turned his head. "I'm awake," he mumbled and sat up, swinging his legs over the platform and onto the packed mineral floor. Finnegan waved to the empty doorway. "It's okay, Monty, I'm up."

A pale face with wide, green eyes peeked around the cave opening. There were no doors to close, so everyone respected each other's sleeping space as best they could. Of course, for a young one born in captivity, life was still an adventure.

"Hi." Montana slid into the doorway now that Finnegan was off his sleeping platform. "Will you tell me a story of Earth again today?" She bounced on the balls of her feet.

Finnegan wished he could just slip into the dream world and never wake up again. One of these days, he'd follow some of the others and go insane, but until then, it was Montana—and fragile ones like Helen—that kept him going. He felt they needed him, more than he needed rest. He reached out and let Monty slip her small warm hand into his, and they moved out into the walkway together.

"Where's George today?"

The girl shrugged, appearing to give no thought at all to his question. Finn shook his head, shaking away thoughts of Montana's father. They moved together along the wide channel, their bare feet never cold on the compact ground beneath them. He had yet to comprehend how the temperature and light always remained exactly the same. All he knew was that he needed a change of some sort, this constant sameness was not meant for humans.

"...to the museum?"

Finn blinked. "Sorry, what?" He had zoned out again, which was happening more often of late. Maybe madness was seeping in.

Monty released his large gentle hand. "Can we go down to the museum, silly." She skipped past room after room without paying attention to them, or the people inside.

"Do you want to see if Helen will come too?"

"Yes!" Monty clapped and raced off.

He couldn't help but smile at her obvious excitement. It really was the kid that gave him hope for the future. If a child with so much spirit and vigor could be born in underground caves, never knowing sunlight or freshwater—or even food for that matter—and still show joy, well it spoke to something within himself.

A few other people passed them in the corridor. Some nodded acknowledgment, while others kept their heads down, eyes on the ground. Finnegan understood the want to never look up again, and the thought drew his eyes up. The transparent ceiling above showed the full, flat, grey underside of the "slugs" as the humans named them, while they slid around above, always watching.

A shudder ran down his spine, and he aimed his sight toward the corridor ahead.

Monty pulled Helen by the arm. Helen was planted firm in the doorway of her room, her eyes blank, seeing right through Monty into her own world. "Come on, Helen." The child tugged harder. "The museum is fun."

"Perhaps we should let her rest today," Finn suggested as he approached the scene. Helen did not look well. She was sinking deeper and deeper every day.

Monty gave Helen's arm a wiggle. Her jade eyes reflected bland beiges of their surroundings and pierced his heart. "But I love Helen, and I want her to smile again."

Finnegan took the girl's small hand out of Helen's slack one, back into his own, and crouched to her level. He turned his knees to keep his sack-dress from exposing himself to the child. "I know you do, and I love her too." He glanced up at Helen's pale oval face, recalling the days when her laughter would fill the room. "You must understand it's hard for us older people." He chucked her under the chin. "That's why it's important for you to hear about Earth. So you can keep sharing the stories as you grow older, and no one will ever forget."

Excited again, Monty jumped up and down. "Okay, let's go," she squealed and was gone.

"They can't see you in the doorway, you know," Helen whispered and closed her eyes.

Finnegan stood at the sound of her voice and planted a gentle kiss on her cheek. "I know, Helen, I know."

He left her to her hiding place and moved off to find Monty.

~~~~~

The "Earth Museum," as the survivors called it, was a large area that housed everything they had brought with them on their ship. Each time Finnegan stepped into the museum, the irony tore at his heart, for the ship's name was Gaia, the mythological personification of Mother Earth. He shook off the "what ifs" that plagued his mind; these thoughts only led down a darker rabbit hole. The past was unchangeable. He could only live for today—or more accurately be alive today, because he certainly would not call this living.

"How do you know ours was the only ship to make it?" Monty asked as Finn approached. Her face was pressed against the thick transparent wall that housed the entire console of Gaia's flight deck. The front of the ship was laid out in the cave, from the nose to the back of the twenty-four crew seats. It sat silent and useless, taunting.

"I've told you already, each of the twelve ships went off to a different planet that might be habitable. Earth was dying, and we could no longer live there. Therefore, we needed to find a planet that we could repopulate with humans and try again."

Monty looked up into his face, and her brow furrowed. "Yeah, but it didn't turn out so well for us. How do you know another ship didn't come here too?"

"You got me. I don't know. I can't know. We're...God only knows how deep underground. I can only share the past and what we can see now. Come on, let's go to the art gallery."

"Can't we go to the canteen? I want to see the food again."

Finn drew a breath as his mind immediately went to the old diner back home, with its yellow Formica tables, bright red plastic seats, and the handwritten menu across a blackboard. His mouth watered at the thought of a cheeseburger, the bun lightly toasted—sprinkled with sesame seeds—and a side of golden fries. He clenched his teeth, biting back the memories. "Not today, please. I can't do it today." He buried the memories of food. It was not necessary here, only a missing pleasure for the human psyche. One that Montana would never know. Down here, they received a pill once a day that somehow sustained their health and replaced the need for even water. The worst was the memory of food, in particular for the binge eaters, the junk-food junkies, and the foodies.

    Finnegan watched the people wander about, some talking in groups or pairs, some staring into the caverns of all they had left of humanity. He noticed there seemed to be fewer people lately, and he didn't know if they were slowly dying off or just not leaving their rooms anymore. By his calculations, and from watching Montana being born and grow, she would be about seven now. There was no way to track time underground. They had no clocks, no difference of night or day. It was always just light, though they didn't know where the light source emanated from. The air was fresh and yet warm, which they were thankful for because they had no blankets or clothes, other than the dresses—which were all identical, only mixed sizes to choose from.

    Monty sighed and saw the pained expression on Finn's face. "Okay, art gallery. Race ya!" She squealed and took off again.

A thin woman, with a steep hunch to her back, lifted her eyes as Monty raced by and shook her head. "Ah, to be that naive."

Finn nodded as he passed and thought, *A brain injury right about now would suffice.*

The corridor was twenty feet wide with vast caverns both left and right, where they could view the last of their belongings. Like the ceiling, the material was transparent, although it wasn't glass. No matter how hard you banged on it, it didn't reverberate as glass would. It was solid as stone, yet see-through. People had been able to commit suicide in the beginning by running headfirst into the walls, and even that didn't crack the material. But they quickly learned that the aliens would not abide by suicide, or murder, and stopped trying.

Finn ran his fingers along the walls as he walked on, always curious as to what exactly what type of material they were. *Perhaps that was what keeps me sane, my need to know and understand. Who are the creatures above? Why had they not just killed us all? Why go to all the trouble of letting us live here, with our belongings just out of reach?* He looked up again to the underside of the "slug" that followed him. He could tell it was the same one by the small blue mark on its tail shaped like an anchor. He had even named it "Tattoo." It was the only one he'd ever seen with this type of mark. The others largely looked identical to each other. They were different sizes and some variation in the color of their undersides, but no other had the blue anchor.

As Finn rounded the bend to the art gallery, he saw an unfamiliar young lady leaning over Monty. Her long dark hair hid her face, but when she spotted his approach, she squeezed Monty's shoulder and hurried off in the opposite direction.

"Who was that?"

"That was Dartania. She usually stays in the ladies' part but was here when I came in. Why did we keep people pictures anyways?"

He could only smile at Monty's attention span. She had not picked up on his curiosity, so he let it go. "Well, back on Earth, art was a way to express one's self. These paintings were created by some of the most famous artists throughout history. We preserved, uh, that means saved," he said, trying to teach her vocabulary as he spoke, "them on the ships, so they would be remembered forever. Each ship had a variety of famous artists to be spread across the universe." He pointed to a small painting of a handsome woman with a hint of a smile. "That one is called the Mona Lisa, painted by Leonardo da Vinci in the 1500s."

Monty's freckled nose crinkled as she took in the picture. "I don't understand art. What's so great about a lady that's not even smiling nicely? And that one..." She bounced over a few places. "It's just blue, why?"

"Well that's the artist, Yves Klein. I can only tell you what I recall from school, but I believe that it was the artist's way of rebelling about some of his other work being misunderstood. Rebelling is doing something against all the rules. For example, instead of him painting a person, he makes just color and says to the world 'this is my art.'"

"Huh, that's weird. But the blue is pretty. It would be nice to have some of this art in my room, then I could stare at them always."

Finnegan placed his hand on her slender shoulder. He could feel her bones against his palm. Sadness welled in his heart again; this was no way for a child to grow up. Not wanting Monty to sense his emotion, he nudged her and pointed ahead. "We're coming up to your favorite."

"Oh, yes. It's bright. I like the bright ones." She scurried forward and pressed her nose against the see-through wall.

They stood before a vibrant colored-pencil drawing of a chameleon, by Morgan Davidson. "Amazing that someone could make that with pencils." He awed, not for the first time, while her eyes darted back and forth, taking in every detail of the picture.

"So pretty," she whispered as her fingers traced lines across the stone.

They moved on past painting after painting, a small tribute to what was left of humanity. Finnegan enjoyed keeping his mind occupied by teaching Monty about life before the underground prison.

"Can you tell me about where my parents were from again?" she asked, grasping one of his large fingers in her own tiny ones.

Finn felt her warmth and wondered if there would ever be more children created. Since they landed on Kepler, Monty was the last child born. Finn nudged her forward. "Of course, let's keep walking."

He led her along the wall of art as he remembered Wendy. She had gotten pregnant before the landing. She was able to carry the child through the full nine months but sadly died at Monty's birth. It had been a shipside fling with George Carlisle, who had no investment in Wendy or the prospect of a child. Therefore, since Montana's birth, many of the people in the caves felt responsible for the little girl and all chipped in to help her develop as normally as they could in these circumstances.

"Your mom was from the state called Montana—"

"And Mom named me after home!"

"Yes, that's right, because home was beautiful and so are you. Your mom grew up on a ranch." He pointed to the painting of lush green grass with the backdrop of the Rocky Mountains. Every time they walked along here, she asked about her mother, and he had no problem repeating the stories. "It would have looked much like this picture. She had horses to ride and a stream to fish in." He tousled her delicate curls. "You would have loved to play there."

Suddenly, their attention was drawn to the sound of men yelling from down the corridor. It was an unusual sound to hear, as there was never arguing or yelling. The voices echoed off the cavern walls, carrying grunts and groans of an actual scuffle.

"Stay here." He pressed Monty to the wall then turned and raced down the path.

His fears were realized as he came around the corner and upon two men in a full-fledged fight.

"Whoa! What's going on?" he called, aiming to distract before the "slugs" intervened. He recognized both men but only knew the name of one, a man that lived on the same level, so he addressed him. "Paul? Paul!"

Paul Smythe grappled the smaller man into a headlock, and as he turned to Finnegan's voice, the unnamed man took the chance to raise his fist and catch Paul square on the nose. Blood burst forth, and Paul dropped his grip as he instinctively grabbed his nose. "ARGH. Now I'm gonna kill you!" He lunged at the smaller man, who had fallen to his knees.

It was too late. A mist streamed in from above their heads.

"Ah, no." Paul stumbled away from the supine man, moaning.

Finnegan knew it was going to happen, and he, too, turned but to head back to Monty to try to shield her from the gas. He covered his nose and mouth with his sack-dress as he staggered toward her.

The gas filled the corridor quickly, and Finn's eyes began to water. There was little he could do. He just wanted to cover Monty so she wouldn't inhale too much. They had no idea what the gas was or how it may affect them long term. His foot twisted, and his eyes closed. The thin fabric wasn't enough to stop the effects of the gas. His eyes closed as the hard ground met him.

2. Changes

Finnegan blinked. He couldn't tell how long he'd been out. He only knew he was back in his bunk. The gas left no lingering headache or dry mouth. He felt at peace. He was thankful for that.

The fight floated back to his memory. He wondered what had happened. Would the men be back in their respective bunks? Or would they be two more casualties of "never to be seen again?" Finn wanted to know, so he left his room and came back through the corridors that led to Paul's compartment.

Others were also starting to roust out of their cubbies. Most people were confused as to why they were gassed, some rubbing sore spots from where they fell and bumped their heads or scraped knees, not being prepared for the knockout. Then he thought he'd better check on Montana first, make sure she was okay.

Finnegan followed the winding corridor as it wove downward.

"Finn!" a voice called from an offshoot hallway.

"What?" He halted and turned to see Helen, her eyes deep lipid pools that currently appeared more doe-like than human.

"Why did they gas us this time? We have been good, haven't we?" Her mouth formed a tight line, her once thick mass of shiny hair, now a rat's nest of tangles.

"It's all right, Helen." He moved to take her in his arms, but she grimaced and pulled back. Finn spoke softly as though to calm a skittish colt. "We're fine, Helen. There was a scuffle between a couple of men. It's nothing to be concerned with." He touched her arm delicately, and she visibly relaxed. He moved in to wrap her in an embrace. He felt her skeleton through her thin shift and rubbed her back soothingly. "Shhh…you're okay. It's all right."

Tears dripped from Helen's eyes, falling onto Finn's neck and tickling his back as they rolled under his shift. "I don't think I can take any more of this, Finn."

"I know, sweetie. I know." He planted a soft kiss on her warm neck and was instantly taken back to the day they made love for the first time. Her skin had been taut, blemish-free, and an olive tone. She had smelled of fresh cotton, and her neck, at that point, was flushed with passion. He let his lips linger, and she stepped back, pushing him away. A look of disgust distorted her gaunt face.

"Forgive me, Helen, I—"

Helen screamed then, her hands clenched into white-knuckled fists, her mouth stretched wide, and the sound she let loose was a shrill vibration of madness.

Finnegan rushed forward, trying to make her stop. He grabbed her by the shoulders, shaking her gently. He wanted to slap her cheek and bring her back from the brink, but he couldn't hit her. He could never imagine hitting her.

"Helen, Helen." His spittle flew into her face.

His efforts were to no avail; she kept right on screaming.

Finn covered his ears. "Stop!" He dropped to his knees as the corridor once again filled with gas. He gave it another try. "Helen." He coughed, and his eyes began to close. "Sto…"

~~~~~~

Helen giggled as he dipped her with a spin. Her head lay back, showing off her long neck. The sound of Johnny Rivers' gentle voice singing "Swayin' to The Music" from 1977, reverberated through the cabin. Helen liked listening to any music that came before the twentieth century. She said it had more meaning to it. Finnegan never argued. If Helen was happy, he was happy.

Her body felt warm and pliable against his, and his heart overflowed with love for her. He never would have imagined that love was a real thing until he met Helen. He pulled her tight to his chest. His lips lingered over her soft skin as he allowed her clean aroma to fill his head. Suddenly, a sense of dread entered his mind.

This time, his eyes flew open. Once again, he was back in his bunk. *How do they do that?* He sat up and checked himself over. He had no lacerations or bruises.

"Goddammit, Helen. Why did you have lose it now?" he spoke aloud to his empty chamber.

Once again, he went back out to the corridor with the intention to check on Helen and then Monty. As he passed by others, he noted the confusion on their faces, and some huddled together in their small rooms, whispering. *Of course they're confused. Two gassings back to back. We haven't been gassed in ages.*

Finnegan headed quickly to Helen's pod. As he neared her space, he slowed, yet his heart raced. He peeked around the corner and prayed to find her still asleep, but as he feared, her room was empty.

"Oh, Helen." Deflated, he slouched against the wall and closed his eyes. He hated what this life was doing to them, stripping away their humanity and will to live. A tear formed in his eye; he knew he'd never see Helen again. He wanted to sink to his knees and scream at the top of lungs like she had. He wanted it to all be over, but Montana popped into his head. Her bright smile and lilting laugh. What would happen to Monty?

"Go find her," he said to himself and forced himself back up to his feet.

Just then, the smaller man from the fight with Paul Smythe came running around the corner. As his head swiveled in Finnegan's direction, he noted the black eye.

"Hey." Finn stepped away from the wall to block the man's passage.

The man halted, lifted his arm as if to avoid another blow, and then he back stepped. "What?"

"Easy now. I just want to know what happened before, between you and Paul I mean." Finn stretched his arm out, narrowing the hallway. "After all, there is nothing left to fight over. Is there?"

The man's eyes widened. His head began to vibrate back and forth. His thinning hair floated comically above his head like a fuzzy halo. "Nah. Un-uh. I'm not falling for that again." He spun and retreated the way he had come, leaving Finnegan bewildered.

From down the corridor, voices reverberated back to him, people saying "watch out" and "hey," so he figured the guy had perhaps lost it and would be the next to disappear.

Moving past the situation, Finnegan went through the center of the common areas and cut around to Montana's cave. She wasn't there, so he went to the next one over where her father slept. "George?"

A grunt floated from within the small space, so Finn stepped into the doorway. "Have you seen Monty since the last gassing?"

George Carlisle lay on his platform with his arms across his chest. He didn't even open his eyes. "Nope."

"Did you at least hear her leave?"

Now one eye peeked open, the black pupil trained on Finnegan. "Where the fuck do you think she's going to go? That's what I'd like to know."

Finn wasn't going to have this conversation again. "She is still a child, George." He walked away before his own ire rose to the point of them all getting gassed again.

A couple of ladies walked past, discussing shoes. "Finn," they greeted and kept going.

He couldn't help but smile. Women would never change. Five minutes later and he'd made the circuit of the community caves, where Monty frequently hung out. He'd asked a couple of people if they'd seen her, but all said no, and no one seemed as concerned as he.

Over the past few years, and his many miles of walking around in circles, he deduced their space was laid out in a grid-like fashion. All the rooms ran east to west, and all passageways between the areas were north and south—or vise versa. Direction was hard to tell when you were miles deep under a strange planet's surface. Now, he had to wonder if she would go back to the museum or perhaps even the women's area.

As he passed the community church, he looked in. Even 32.5 million miles from Earth, held captive underground like ants, some humans still needed the security of a false god. Pastor Mayweather was preaching as people sat on the floor, listening intently, but there was no child. He kept going. Every so often he'd turn his head and look into someone's room—it was hard not to without doors—but still no Monty.

He arrived at Paul Smythe's room and ducked his head around the corner. "Hi, Paul."

[25]

Paul sat up. He'd been lying down but must not have been sleeping. "Finn, what's up?"

"Have you seen Montana?"

"Nope, sorry."

Finnegan chewed at the inside of his cheek. He knew there was nowhere to go but was worried nonetheless. He had not considered the slugs would have taken her—there had been no reason to—but now it was a seed in his mind. "Tell me then, what was that fight about earlier?"

"Ever wonder if they piss and shit?"

"Pardon?"

Paul's eyes rolled upward as his head stayed locked in place. "You can't see any holes on their undersides. And, well, we don't shit and piss anymore. It's funny, but I miss taking a good healthy dump, don't you?" Paul hopped off his platform and paced. His hands fluttered about punctuating his words. "Oh, man, that makes me think of a nice juicy steak and a cold beer. What I wouldn't give for a frosty one, huh! And how is it possible that our hair or nails no longer grow? I mean look at them." He held his hands out. "What, six or seven years, and we don't have beards to our knees or hair down our backs? It's just not right." Paul began to pace and recant a tale from Earth days. He had been a heavy equipment mechanic and was a large, burly man. Now in the underground caves of Kepler, he still exuded that rugged manly demeanor, even though his cheeks were gaunt.

Finnegan watched the tall man as he stomped back and forth in his small empty cave and thought, *What is going on? Is everyone losing it at once?* "Well, perhaps we should talk later..." he said aloud, and he began to turn when he noticed Paul mouthing words.

Finn looked up at the clear ceiling. Tattoo was there but also two other larger slugs. He looked back at Paul, who was imitating a badly dubbed kung-fu movie. He was ranting about food, hunger, and sex, but in between his speech, there were other words. Silent, unspoken words. Finnegan moved into the room acting enthralled by the man's crazy ranting but concentrated on his mouth.

Paul gestured wildly. "There was this" *meet* "tall brunette" *at* "oh boy, let me" *west*, "tell you, she" *steam* "had a body" *four* "that I" *hours* "could fuck for days!"

Finnegan picked out the mouthed-only words: "Meet at west steam four hours." He motioned that he understood the coded message. "Okay, Paul, thanks for the story, but I have to go find Monty."

Paul stopped pacing. "I get it. Go find her. I'll see you later, right?"

Finn nodded and gave him a thumbs-up. He interpreted the code, but he did not understand it. Not by a long shot.

He resumed his trek around through the tunnels, asking everyone he passed whether or not they'd seen Monty. It wasn't as though she was a stranger; they all knew the only child in their prison. It had to have been at least an hour since the last gassing, and Finn was starting to panic. He stopped near another common room to look in, and instead found himself looking up. "Where is she?"

Tattoo stopped along with Finn. It hovered on the transparent ceiling above him, unmoving.

Just then, a woman came around the bend. "Uh, Finn?" she questioned.

He rubbed his face, sighing. If Monty was gone, he wanted them to take him next. He needed to know where the people went when they disappeared. Even if it meant the end, without Helen or Monty, he was ready for that. He finally acknowledged the woman before him. "What, Brenda?" He was blunt with her, a warning to keep her distance.

Brenda's eyes narrowed, and her mouth pulled down into a deep frown. "I heard you were looking for Monty is all…but if I'm bothering you…" She hesitated knowingly.

Finn stepped into her frail body, bumping his knee inadvertently against hers. He had to control the urge to grasp her bony shoulders and give her a hard shake. "You know where she is?"

Brenda blinked in surprise at his outburst. "Yeah." She moved a step back, hunching her shoulders protectively. "She's in the women's area with Dartania." Then she reached for him. "Do you want me to go get her?"

"Sorry, for…" Finn shook his head. He couldn't apologize to Brenda under any circumstances, or she'd start hounding him again, and down here there was nowhere to hide. "No. I'll be fine. Someone will get her for me." Without waiting for a reply, he jogged away from her.

He felt a weight lift from his shoulders, knowing at least Monty was safe. As he jogged through the tunnels, passing pod after pod, he realized Brenda had said Monty was with that girl, Dartania. Odd how someone he had never seen before was suddenly the center of this day—or night, who knew? Now he wished he'd asked Brenda about this other woman.

He decided it still wasn't worth the further repercussions that would follow.

~~~~~~~

In the early days of waking up captive underground, Finn had spent most of his time walking. He had followed every path, every twist, and entered many rooms. Their new "ant colony" of a home was nothing but tunnels, with single sleeping pods, odd-sized common rooms, and the hot sauna rooms. He had walked, ran, and jogged through it all, desperate for a way out. Their ship had held five hundred thousand people, and they were all here, or those who had survived were here, and there was no escape. All the trails eventually circled back to his own sleeping pod, and eventually, he gave up wandering. Everything was an exact repeat of itself, other than the people. He knew the women-only area was approximately three miles from the museum. It was the only place he'd never explored—obviously not a woman. But he had been reassured it was no different than anywhere else. There had been strong women, opinionated women, women liberals, sexual assault victims, and plain man-haters that had formed an alliance and taken a "men banished" area for their own. Finn never cared, and he wasn't sure why they did either. There was no longer sexual desire for anyone, another pleasant life-altering change made by their captors. He made his way there now to find Montana.

Once he arrived, he sat against the wall near the opening to the women's space and closed his eyes. He'd hear if anyone approached. He was transported back to the day Gaia crashed.

They knew going to strange new planets was a risk, but they had no choice. Earth was dead. Upon arrival, they'd discovered their plan was defunct; they had not expected Kepler to have no atmosphere. It should not have mattered. Gaia was equipped to keep all five hundred thousand people in cryostasis for upward of a thousand years. The plan changed from landing on Kepler to just orbiting the planet, along with its two suns, in stasis. Everyone would return to sleep and wait for word from one of the other twelve Earth ships, and then they'd be off once again.

Finn pulled Helen into his arms. They spent one last day together awake on the ship. He had planned a date night and booked the observation room, where the movie dome showed the entire strange, starry sky of their choosing. They lay amongst a downy bed of faux furs, wrapped naked in each other's arms. Helen purred in his ear as he made passionate love to her, unknowingly their last time. When the movie was off, they could see Kepler's brown dead surface miles below, while Barry White crooned for them. As the next day dawned, Finn tucked Helen into her hibernation chamber with one last warm kiss goodnight. He returned to his bed vowing to dream of her until their next awaking, no matter how many years away that may be.

However, when they did wake, it was not to the tune of a sister ship to the rescue but to an alien world, underground, left with nothing but a sea of humanity.

Even now, remembering those nights with Helen, he felt no stirring in his loins. They were stripped of everything that made people *people*, and it was soul-crushing. His eyes fluttered. He didn't want to remember anymore, and now he may never see Helen again.

"What are you doing out here?"

A voice broke into his thoughts. Finnegan opened his eyes looking up at Mark Jones, a fellow botanist that had worked with Helen on Gaia. He raised his hand, and the other man instinctively reached down and helped him to his feet. "I'm waiting for Montana. Someone said she went into the women's area."

Mark nodded. "I heard Helen was taken. I'm sorry, man." He shook his head. "Two gassings in one day. Something is not right."

"None of this is right."

"No." Mark shifted his weight and crossed his arms. His elbows stuck out, pointed and gangly. He had already been a lean man, but the life-sustaining pills did nothing to build muscle or fat. Unless they worked out consistently, which Mark did not, it left most people skeletal. "I mean, things are changing," he finished with a twitch of his head.

Finn stepped closer to Mark, knowing that Tattoo was still above. It had gotten the point where he could sense the slug. Even if he ran, it was almost always there, keeping pace. His curiosity was piqued, however. "What is different now from every other day? If we have days and nights, who can tell with this never-ending light."

"Well for starters, the double gassing—"

Finn scoffed. "I'll tell you I was fortunate enough to be there for both of them."

"Oh." Mark perked up, interested now that there was some news to hear. "What happened?" He picked at a scab on one of his bony elbows.

"The first time was because of two men fighting. I only heard the fight go down. I didn't make it there in time to stop it or question anyone, and then we were back in our chambers as usual. And the second one was Helen losing it." He shook his head, remembering the look on Helen's face when he'd tried to kiss her. "It's all my fault."

Mark shook his head. "It's this place, man." The creases in his face deepened. "How much longer do you think we can live like this before we're all nutjobs? Anyone who is not strong enough"—he tapped his temple— "will go mad first. At least you had Helen for all this time. Count your lucky stars."

"Yeah, aren't we lucky."

"One day we'll be rescued. They're coming for us." Mark had picked the scab off, and now blood was trickling down his arm.

Finn raised an eyebrow; Mark was acting strangely. He was about to ask if he was all right when Monty came strolling out of the cave.

"Hi, Finn."

He spun from his conversation. "You scared the life out of me, Montana! Why did you just disappear like that?"

She shrugged unconcernedly. "When I woke up, Dartania was in my room and asked me to come with her."

Finn pulled her to his hip, giving her a rough hug. "Please don't ever do that again. Tell someone, anyone, where you are going." He looked down into her wide jade eyes. He stared at her, memorizing the spattering of tawny freckles that dotted her cheeks.

He was burning her image into his mind, so if anything ever happened, he would never forget. "I was worried they took you is all."

"Sure, I didn't think it mattered. I have nowhere else to go."

While it was true that Finn knew there were other levels with many people Montana had never met, it wasn't people he worried about.

As they were talking, Mark had slipped away.

They headed back toward their familiar area. "Why did Dartania want you to go with her?"

Out of habit, Monty slid her small, warm hand into his as they walked. "She wants me to move to the lady area with her."

Finn's heart skipped a beat. He just lost Helen; he couldn't lose Monty too. "Really? Whatever for? I mean, it must be exactly the same as everywhere else."

"Well, it's sort of different. But I don't want to go, Finn. I like being near you and Helen and Alma and the museum."

Oh no, he hadn't thought about the fact that Monty didn't know Helen was gone. He hadn't even thought about Alma, who acted as a grandmother figure to Monty. She, too, would be heartbroken that Helen had been taken from them. He wasn't ready yet to deal with the emotions. "It's a long walk back to our area. Do you want to hear another Earth tale?"

"Can you tell me about the end again?"

She was a too enthusiastic for Finn's taste. He understood though. All she ever knew were caverns and people. She never tasted a cherry pie or had the wind blow her hair, or lay staring at the stars and dreaming about the unknown universe. He sighed. Remembering was torture and bliss.

3 Earth's Demise

Finnegan recounted the demise of Earth to Montana as they ambled back toward their pods, Tattoo sliding silently along overhead, following every step.

"Ironically it was 2999—"

Monty wiggled Finn's arm. "Iron-ik-what?"

"In the year 1999, people had the strange idea that when the year changed to 2000, all the computers in the world would stop working." He chuckled. Being a computer programmer himself, he couldn't believe that this part of history was real. Sadly, it was, and it made the people of that era come across as simple-minded. He was glad to have been born almost a thousand years later. "Therefore, it's funny, and not ha-ha funny but coincidental funny—ironic—that in 2999 the actual earth would die."

Monty nodded. Finn knew she was still too young to understand irony, but he'd remember to find other examples until she did.

He resumed his tale. "Anyway, the people of Earth had been trying to change their ways for hundreds of years.

They learned how to stop boring holes and siphoning oil from underground. They built big towers that harnessed the wind for power. They used other machines in the ocean to obtain power from the waves. They stopped using chemicals that were killing animals and insects, and it was all working. The earth, though overpopulated, was rebuilding itself to sustain life as long as we worked with her and not against her."

"I sure would like to see an ocean one day," Monty mumbled.

Finn ignored the comment, wanting that for them both as well. "The one thing we could never change was the dying sun. If you remember, the sun was a giant star that we relied on for heat, light, and life. It would warm the earth and help plants and people grow. We knew without it, all the food would die, and the earth would get freezing cold and winter would come." He looked down at Monty, wondering if she could even grasp any of these concepts, of heat, cold, plants. "In 2966, when I was five, the sun started to show signs of cooling. I was raised to study computers so that when the time came, I could be a part of the evacuation of the earth."

"Did the sun completely die?"

"Not yet it hadn't. But the scientists calculated that it only had a few hundred years left. If they were right—humans are never one hundred percent right," he ruminated, "the earth was already feeling the cold anyway. Our average temperature had dropped by four degrees, and the northern hemisphere was experiencing longer winters and no summer, only a few warmer months. As soon as the smartest people on the planet were able to build spaceships that were capable of carrying hundreds of thousands of people—"

"But not every person on Earth went, right? I remember this part. You said lots of people had to stay."

"That's right." He gave her a gentle squeeze. "Going on these space trips was expensive, and not everyone could afford to pay. Some of us, like your mom, Helen, and Alma were workers on the ships. Others could fly them, and some paid for passage. Also, there will always be people too set in their ways to change. They don't want to go traipsing off into outer space and would rather stay with their homes and families."

Even though dying with Earth would have been a better life choice than this, Finn could not regret the time he had in deep space and the love he'd found with Helen. Had he stayed on Earth, he would have died alone in his cabin, never knowing what it meant to love a woman. Thoughts of Helen made him sad again, so he focused on his story. "Now, we knew that we were going to land on Kepler in the year 3314, that's three hundred fifteen years after leaving Earth. We have no way to judge time here and can only really go by your growth. If we calculate from your birth in 3314, and you appear to be seven years old, we are in approximately the year 3321. Therefore, the earth is most likely dead now.

"That's kind of sad."

They were nearing the Earth Museum; his story was long enough to get them back to their area. "Are you tired?"

"Nah, I'm okay."

"Let's go visit Alma."

"Yes," Monty squealed and took off running.

Finn sighed and thought, *Enjoy every second of happiness, Montana*, knowing his bad news was going to tear her apart.

With a heavy heart, Finn rounded to corner to Alma's pod, preparing himself to break the news—that Helen was taken—to the last two important ladies in his life.

He jolted to a stop as he entered the threshold to find Montana sitting in Helen's lap. "Helen!" He rushed to the platform, throwing his arms around her and Monty, squeezing them tight together.

[40]

Monty squealed, wriggled out of his crushing grasp, and jumped to the floor.

Helen laughed. "Are you okay, Finnegan?" She patted his arm.

"No, I thought I lost you forever." He held her at arm's length, checking her over. "What happened? Where did they take you? What was it like up there?" He rushed on.

Helen's brow furrowed, and she pushed Finn off. "What are you on about?"

Concerned, Alma touched Finnegan's shoulder. "Why are you asking these questions, Finn? Do you think something happened to Helen?"

"Uh?" Finn looked between the three women, seeing the worry on their faces. He knew what he saw, or thought he saw. *Maybe Helen wasn't taken but came to Alma's immediately after waking up?* He smiled and sat on the platform beside Helen. "I'm an idiot." He shook his head. "After the last gassing, I went to check on you"—he addressed Helen— "and you were gone, I thought they took you away. I am just happy to find you here. You have no idea the thoughts!"

Alma clutched her chest. "That's a relief. I wasn't sure if you were losing it on us, Finnegan." She brought Monty to her side in a comforting hug. "Well, Helen and I have been together for about the last hour-ish…" She shrugged in the who-can-tell-time-down-here gesture. "But that last knockout was hours ago. Why is it taking you so long to check?"

Finn looked closer at Helen. Her hair was no longer tangled, and she had a slight smile on her lips. The last time he saw her, she'd been hollow-eyed, and he had not seen her smile in months. He thought about the timeline. *From his pod to Helen's, to his search for Monty, the wait at the women's area, and the trek back here, four hours must have passed. Should he relay this to Alma or wait and see if Helen had any other odd changes?* He smiled and told them the truth. "Monty had disappeared, so I went off to find her, all the way over to the women's section no less." He knew that would distract them.

As they began to fuss over Monty and question her motives, Finn realized that approximately four hours had passed, and he needed to go. He leaned in and gave Helen a quick hug then did the same to Alma and Monty. "I told some guys I'd meet them for a steam. Keep an eye on this one, okay?"

Helen nodded, taking Monty's hand in her own. "Of course. We always do."

~~~~~~

After Finnegan left, Alma watched Helen laughing with Monty. She knew what he had been talking about but held her tongue. She didn't want to worry Helen or scare the child. She also knew that this was not the first time Helen had gone away and been returned happier. It had been a few years, she figured, and Finnegan had not seen it happen back then.

"...favorite food?" Monty's small voice penetrated Alma's musing.

Helen swooped Monty up into her arms. "Let's not talk about that. Let's go over to the museum and look at clothes." She swung Monty around until her hair lifted.

Monty giggled, letting out a loud whoop.

"That sounds like a nice idea." Alma laughed along with them, keeping her eyes trained on Helen. "We'll play pretend dress-up, come on."

As they moved out to the corridor, Alma wondered if she should confide in Finn or not. Would it help their situation any? As a lifelong counselor, it was in her nature to observe first and speak later. She decided to watch Helen further, ask her different questions, and do some research before alarming Finn.

Monty's small hand found her own, and Alma smiled down at the girl. It felt nice to have someone naive about the earth around. Alma was never one to own possessions, other than expensive clothes, and she never thought about money. Her philosophy was that love made a life, and here they were, all stripped bare of everything but emotion. She'd never been more content.

"I love you," Alma said to the child.

~~~~~~

Finnegan walked back past his pod and the all-too-familiar museum sights as he headed to the steam cavern to meet with Paul. He couldn't believe that after years of nothing exciting happening, *ever*, he was having a stressful day. First Helen disappears and reappears, or at least in his mind she had, then Monty takes off to the women's area. This Dartania character was spotted twice, after never being seen before. And now the men have some secret meeting. It was shaping up to be quite the day. He felt a smile creep up; stress was better than nothingness.

As he entered the steam cavern, voices echoed around the space, all muffled and blended together. The cavern was oval in shape. The doorway was lower. Finn had to duck to enter, and he wasn't sure if it was carved this way or was a natural formation. The steam, unlike the sulfurous earth magma, was odorless. It emanated up through fissures along the outer edges of the space, so everyone gathered near the center. There appeared to be five men in the room, who were sitting in a circle talking quietly. They stopped talking, and two men shuffled back to allow him space. As he sat, he saw George was one of the group, and he frowned.

"Glad you came." Paul nodded. "We are going to need all the help we can get."

Finn cocked his head. "Help with what?"

"We have a plan to get the hell out of this dump," George exclaimed too loudly.

The others all shushed him, and Finn caught himself naturally looking up at the ceiling, but of course, the idea was that the ceiling in the steam room was never clear. He thought he could make out the underside of his pal, Tattoo, but even that was blurred.

George harrumphed and crossed his arms. "You think they can even understand what we say? I highly doubt it. They're bloody slugs for Christ's sake!"

"We don't know if they can or can't. Do we?" Russell chipped in, pointing his stubby finger at George. "We've been here for what...six, seven years? And we still know nothing. But we do know they have control." Russell had been one of Gaia's pilots, but now he was just another body trapped underground.

Finn angled his head toward George. "Why is he here? I can't see how he has anything to contribute."

Paul cleared his throat, commanding everyone's attention. When the chattering stopped, and all eyes were on him, he spoke. "Everyone in this room is here for a reason. Finnegan, it was George who gave us a lead on the way into the museum..."

Finn's jaw dropped as the voices rose again. He swiveled to eye George, unbelieving. It had to be a scam on George's part. He leaned into the circle. "A way into the museum? With Gaia and all our stuff?"

Paul smiled, his teeth still healthy and gleaming white, his baby blues lit up like a kid at

Christmas. "Yes, a way in to our stuff." He waited for the chatter to stop again then resumed speaking. "George overheard a girl telling Bill Davis—uh, that guy I was fighting with earlier. He was refusing to tell me anything. That's why I hit him. Anyway..." Paul waved the fight off like it was nothing. "There is a small opening through one of the tunnels in the women's area that leads deeper underground and into the cabin area of the museum."

"After I was going crazy looking for Monty, and you knew this information." Finn spun on George. He wanted to hit the man. "You should have known she was off with this other woman."

"How the fuck would I know where she was? It's not like she tells me anything," George growled back, his beady eyes barely visible through lowered lids.

Finn hampered his anger, knowing that to hit George would change nothing and only draw more attention to their group. He focused his attention back to Paul. "So up until now, only Bill and George knew?" Finn glanced at the other faces: Russell Emerson, the pilot; Paul Smythe, a mechanic; Preston Haywood, astronomer and guidance system specialist; Bertram Grant, a doctor; himself, a computer expert; and George Carlisle...a nobody. "And you gathered people who you thought we be useful in coming up with an escape plan?" He surmised, "Have you talked to..." He glanced at George. "I'm assuming it was Dartania whom you overheard?"

Paul shook his head. "Not yet, no. We can't seem to approach her, other than Bill for some reason. Whenever a guy approaches her, she runs back into the women's area. I'll need one of you guys"—Paul pointed to the others— "to see if you can talk to Bill and find out what he knows, or convince him to join the group to help."

Bertram Grant cleared his throat. "I can use the excuse of checking out his eye, make sure he doesn't have a concussion, and see if he'll open up to me."

This was reasonable to everyone. It was natural for people to trust doctors. Especially an older, grey-haired, soft-spoken doctor, like Bertram. His role on Gaia had been a simple courtesy to the fellow shipmates, for in this day and age, the technology did all the work. He was just a face to console away the pain and worry.

"Well, clearly we're going to need a few women involved here," Preston interjected. "After all these years, we can't just suddenly go traipsing into that area unnoticed." He pointed at the ceiling.

"Relax." Paul looked around the group. "We've only just learned of this. Perhaps it's not even true…"

That statement raised the volume level again, and he had to shush the men.

"Listen," he growled low. "We have been down here a long time, with no prospects of getting out. Now we have a tiny speck of hope. Let's take our time, be smart and careful. First, we need to know if this chick is telling the truth. Then we need a woman to scope it out, and we'll go from there. We don't want the beasts to get suspicious, if they have brains, therefore we'll have to change up the meetings and who meets when, and so on. Am I clear?"

Finn was taking in all the new and exciting information when a thought occurred to him. "When I found Montana, she was saying that Dartania wanted her to move into the women's area, but not why. Let me talk to her about that." He tapped his chin, thinking, *She must not have seen the entrance yet, or she would have been too excited by it*. He was pulled out of his thought as Bertram stood and said he was going to find Bill Davis.

"But who trusts any of these crazy bitches here?" George grumbled.

"I can talk to Alma Klein," Finn stated, knowing that she was level-headed and trustworthy. He would have to approach her cautiously to keep the secret from Helen. There was just something not right about Helen's disappearance and return, and he knew Alma would want to involve her.

Paul agreed. "Yes, a psychologist will work. She's not overly emotional." He gave Finn a thumbs-up. "Let's start there and wait a few days before we met again. Russell and Preston, I want you guys to start seriously thinking about a way off this planet."

Neither man responded. They glanced at each other, both knowing that the ship was a lost cause, and Paul would know that too. They just did not know if there was a possibility that the aliens of Kepler had their own space travel options. All they could hope for was to get out of the underground system and get to the surface again.

"No talking about any of this outside of the steam rooms," Paul finished, clapping the men next to him on their backs, and stood. "I've sweated enough, let's get out of here."

Finnegan moved away from the circle and propped himself against the stone wall. It was warm and moist from the continuous steam, relaxing the muscles in his upper back. He let his head fall back and closed his eyes. "I'm going to rest here for a bit longer."

The men, except for George, called out their goodbyes and left Finn alone with his thoughts.

4. Days go by

Hours later, people had all settled into their pods to sleep. Finn marveled at the habits of humans and wondered if the aliens had the same type of patterns. Even though down in the hive there was no difference between night and day, and no clocks to watch, people still held their lifelong ritual, awake for approximately sixteen hours and then sleep for eight. Sure, there was the odd person who roamed about regardless of the hour, perhaps they had insomnia or were backward on their timeline. He shook off the useless thoughts. A sure sign of madness. His last thought brought a smile to his face.

He had spent the last couple of hours with Monty, Helen, and Alma, anxious to get Alma alone so he could talk to her about the plan, but it was not to be. He eventually left as Monty climbed onto Helen's platform, asking if she could cuddle for the night. Of course, Helen was overjoyed by the prospect, and they bid goodnight to Finnegan. After returning to his own pod, he did his routine pre-sleep yoga—he found it helped him rest better—and climbed onto his hard platform. His last thought before drifting to sleep was if he would ever get to feel the softness of a mattress again. Blackness overtook him, and dreamland brought him back to the last happiest days of his life.

Helen giggled, and her head tilted left, her chestnut hair reflecting the ambient glow of artificial lighting. She tangled her fingers into Finn's and pulled him along the stark corridor. "It's not much farther, I promise."

Finn couldn't hold back his grin even if he tried. He felt the fool, never having loved before and his normal comfort zone more stoic. He let the delicate creature, with her soft touch and joyous demeanor, take him out of his shell, and he laughed as she led him to her surprise.

They passed a few people, who said hi or nodded, but for the most part, people kept to their own groups and weren't interested in what the two lovebirds were up to. Finnegan recognized this area of Gaia as the botanist's workrooms and, not taking much stock in vegetation, had never before come down this far. He wondered what surprise she could have for him in her workspace.

Finn returned a happy smile as she glanced over her shoulder at him again. His heart was light, regardless of where they were headed.

Helen tapped her thumb against the ID pad, and the door wicked open silently. She never released Finn's fingers. They entered a humid narrow hallway that was encased in bright white glowing walls, the floor under their slipper feet also white. Finn squinted at the difference in ambient light and wondered if this was how they helped grow plants in space.

His mouth dropped open as they exited the hallway, through one more glass door, and into the atrium. His head swiveled left, right, up, and around again. Had he known it looked like this, he would have come here more often. He was essentially in a tropical jungle that was hurdling thousands of miles per hour through outer space.

The walkway under his feet was a soft loam of moss that blended from emerald to lime to pine interlaced with tawny browns and bounced with a delicate spring as they walked over it. They were surrounded on all sides by every variation of tree species that he knew: palm, oak, birch, cedar, pine, maple, and countless ones that Finn could not name. Between all the trees were bushes, flowers, and vegetation. The dome above was clear and showcased the darkness of deep space with the twinkle of stars and the galaxies. Helen laughed as she tugged Finn along while his head whipped around trying to take it all in.

"See," she gently mocked. "I've been trying to get you in here for weeks, and this isn't even the surprise."

"Wow! I…uh…wow…" Finn stammered. "How do you get all these different species to cohabitate? I mean, I'm no expert, but I do know that plants grow in their own regions."

Helen rolled her eyes and continued knowingly around the maze of paths, leading them where she wanted to go. "Technology, dear. Not something I have interest in discussing at the moment."

Finn's gait slowed as he spotted a Venus flytrap that was eight feet tall. Its leaves were bigger than him, and the scary part? The two lobes that would close over its prey were about fifteen feet in diameter. "Please tell me you didn't name that Audrey II?"

"What?" Helen caught Finn's gaze and, in turn, his reference to the old movie Little Shop of Horrors *and laughed. "Well I certainly did not, but it's also not mine. You can ask Mark. It's his. Don't worry, I won't feed you to it—yet."*

He continued to take all the familiar and unique plants in as they rounded the last bend, and the forest of plant life opened to a glade with a strategically formed rock waterfall that flowed into a forty-foot, round pond.

"Why did I never know this was here?" Finn mumbled as he breasted Helen and slipped his arm around her slender waist.

"Because you're a man and refused to watch the ship's intro movie that detailed it all?" She let her head rest against his shoulder as they moved toward the water. "Of course, people can't just traipse through here whenever they want. They have to buy a pass and can only come as observatory groups at set times of day." Helen pursed her lips and explained further. "You know with the plants we have growing here, we have to maintain the integrity of their life and humans' lives too."

Finn harrumphed. "You don't have to tell me. People are assholes and stupid to boot." He aimed a thumb over his shoulder. "I'm sure your plant back there would have a feast."

"Here." Helen pushed against Finnegan's hip, directing him around the pond to a wooden bridge. "Your surprise is…" She let go and raced up the planks to the center of the bridge, then bent and came back up holding two fishing poles.

"There are fish in here?" His grin grew exponentially. One thing he missed most about Earth was the ability to hunt and fish for his own sustainability. He liked being independent of society.

"It's fully stocked with salmon, bass, trout, and more." Helen handed him one rod and kept the other. Already hooked and bobbed, she picked up a small can and popped it open to show him fat, juicy earthworms.

Finnegan grabbed Helen roughly around the shoulders and brought her to his chest so quickly that she almost lost the can to the pond. He planted a sturdy wet kiss on her lips. "I love you!" He laughed heartily and then took the can and placed it to his nose, inhaling the scent. "Mmm, nothing like the smell of fresh worms." His senses transported him back to his ranch and the calm, cool autumn days by the lake, and a tear slid out of his eye.

"*Finn?*" *Helen's smile slipped to a worried frown, and she touched his elbow, saddened now that her surprise may have soured.*

Finnegan opened his eyes and kissed Helen again. "*It's amazingly perfect,*" *he reassured her,* "*the best gift I've ever gotten.*" *He dipped a worm on the crook of his finger and proceed to stab it onto her hook.* "*Sometimes it just hits me that there is no more earth, you know?*"

Helen nodded. "*I do know, Finn. I do.*"

Finn grinned in his sleep. His mouth watered at the savory taste of his freshly caught and perfectly seasoned dinner. As a drip of saliva ran out of the corner of his mouth, he woke up. His eyes took in the transparent ceiling, where an alien creature was hovering. Anger boiled in his stomach.

"What do you want from me?" he questioned the thing without raising his voice. It did not acknowledge that he spoke. It did not move nor respond in any way. "I hate you," he grumbled, sliding off his platform, and stepped over to the tiny hole in the cave wall. He dipped a finger in and came out with his life-sustaining, tasteless, odorless, colorless meal. "The only upside to this life is no longer needing to vacate the bowels." Finn addressed Tattoo. "I really would like to know how you accomplished that one. Cheers." He swallowed the pill.

Finnegan left his pod and headed straight toward Helen's area, not only to see how she was today but to see if he could talk to Monty. He was going to attempt to gather some information about the girl named Dartania. If he could.

~~~~~~

It took two days for Bertram to find Bill Davis, only because the man never seemed to be in his pod. Bertram had even spent a few hours sitting outside the man's sleeping space on the first day, but he never appeared. He just happened to be wandering the corridors when he spotted the straggled wisps of hair that always seemed to wave about Bill's balding head. He was amongst one of the religious gatherings.

Bertram slipped into the back of the room, knees and shoulders bent, as he melded in with the group. "Excuse me," he whispered, tucking between Bill and a slack-faced elderly woman. She grumbled as she pushed over to make space then fell back into her silent stare.

At the front was Pastor Carl Mayweather. He paced, hands held behind his back, speaking bible passages by rote.

Bill's gaze flicked to Bertram, his mouth tightened, and his attention returned to the front.

"Can we talk?" Bertram whispered.

"Shh." Bill pointed at the pastor, clearly intent on hearing the sermon. He nodded and muttered "uh-uh," along with the group.

Bertram looked around the room. He recognized most of the faces from this area and was a bit surprised by some. As a doctor, he was familiar with people taking up religion in the face of sickness, as a means to cope with the unknowable. Yet he was never able to side with them, he allowed his patients to do anything they felt they needed to survive. He just couldn't understand how in this situation any of them would think it helped. However, the pastor's voice was melodic, and he was beginning to feel a comforting peace fall over him. This was a feeling he had not had for some time, and he sighed. Tension released from his shoulders, and his eyes began to close.

"OH." Bertram was startled as his chin hit his chest. He sat up quickly, straightening his back, and glanced around.

"It's over. Come on." Bill had stood, along with many of the others.

Bertram shook his head, suppressed a yawn, and accepted the man's outstretched hand. "Sorry, I guess I was tired."

Bill waited as people gathered into their small groups away from the two men then said, "Why are you here?"

"As a doctor, I was worried," Bertram replied, looking, but not touching, the bruise on the smaller man's face. "I wanted to make sure you were okay. It's not like we get any health care down here." He laughed uncomfortably.

"You're lying..."

Bertram shushed Bill as heads turned. After placing his arm across Bill's shoulder, he drew them farther away from the others. "Well," he said, talking lower, "you know what the others want. Why don't you want to help out?"

"What about them?" Bill glanced upward. "This may not be the life, but I don't want to die."

Bertram nodded his understanding, squinted, and thought about his best approach. "At least tell me, what is your connection with the girl?"

"Oh." Bill was taken aback, not expecting that question. "Dartania Aswar? She's my niece. Good kid, but this..." He waved toward the cavern. "This is messing with her head. She lost her parents in the crash, you know." He continued on, no longer keeping his voice down. "She took off into that place along with the other women not long after we woke up here, and she hardly ever comes out."

Bertram's eyebrows raised at that, and Bill stumbled on. "No, seriously. Sometimes she comes to see me…uh…to check on me, I suppose. I am the only family she has left, you know."

People had moved in closer to the duo, and Bertram took notice. He took a quick glance at the watchers about their heads and decided it was getting too weird. "Come back to the sauna room in a few hours, okay?" He gave Bill's shoulder a tight squeeze. "We really need you, man." His chin flicked up at the people around them. "We all do." He dropped his arm and moved swiftly out of the cavern, leaving Bill to think about what he meant.

~~~~~

The same day Bertram spoke to Bill, Finn didn't find the ladies in any of their pods and went straight to the museum. The three were huddled together at the ship's food display. He hated coming here. He could almost feel his stomach rumble at the mere thought of wanting to taste something again, anything. But his stomach was not hungry, and it was not possible for it to rumble. He gritted his teeth and moved into the group. Montana was talking rapidly as usual.

"…and why would people *have* to eat?" She pressed up against the transparent wall. "We don't *have* to eat now."

"I'll let you try this time." Helen smiled at Alma as she played with Monty's soft curls.

"Well, we do have to give our bodies nutrition to live." Alma watched Finn approach but kept addressing Montana's question. "Here, the slugies take care of us, and that one little pill you take every day, replaces all the food and vitamins that we used to have to intake. The slugies are amazing beings with great resources that we do not understand."

Monty laughed at Alma calling the watchers slugies. "Why don't they just let us eat that food?"

"There is not enough food left in there to sustain all of us for more than a few years."

Helen and Monty spun as Finnegan's voice came from behind them.

He continued. "You see those little silver packets?" Taking her by the shoulders, he turned her back to the window.

She nodded.

"All we would do is add water, and they would plump up three times the size." He exaggerated by holding his hands a foot apart from each other. She laughed again, and Finn smiled back. He loved hearing her high giggle. "And that would be a whole meal, and we had to do that a least twice a day. For oh…" He tapped his chin as he calculated the people. "Five hundred thousand people, give or take. But when we crashed here, part of the storage area got burned up, and the food along with it." His eyes traveled along the blacked wall behind the long cafeteria-style counter.

"Thank you, slugies!" Monty waved at the three forms that hovered above the group.

Finn held back a frown and looked for any reaction from Helen. When she seemed not to care in the slightest that the child was waving to the aliens, he addressed Monty. "Why are you thanking them?

"Well, if they give us vinamis to live, and we don't have our own food, then we'd all die, right?"

"You sure are smart for someone that never went to school, aren't you?" Alma gave a light clap to enforce her joy at the girl's thought process. "And the word is vitamins, but you were close."

Wanting to move away from the area, Finn turned and began talking as he walked away. Without hesitation, the ladies followed him. "Monty, did you tell Alma and Helen about your new friend?"

"Sure, I have," Monty said.

"Oh, who's that?" Helen asked.

"You remember. Dartania, the pretty lady."

Helen nodded. "Ah, yes. The long-haired girl, right?"

"When did you and her start hanging out?" he questioned.

"What's going, Finnegan?" Alma strode faster to get up beside him.

Finn took her elbow gently, her translucent skin downy soft to the touch. "I'm just looking out for Monty is all."

Monty, meanwhile, had scrunched up her face thinking as they rounded a bend closing in on Alma's pod. "Well, before you took me to the movie house room but after the observatory. I think."

Finnegan thought back to how long ago those two museum trips were. He thought perhaps fifteen to twenty sleeps ago. Of course, an exact tracking was impossible. "And have you gone into the ladies-only area often?" This question drew audible intakes from both Helen and Alma. They had not known Monty was going off with this strange woman.

"Na-ha, just twice." Monty bounced on her toes. "You should come! We're girls; we can go there. It mostly looks the same as here, but they have some bigger rooms where they can all sleep together, and they are not as lonely at night. I don't like being alone at night. I have strange dreams."

Helen scooped the girl up into her arms. "I know, baby. That's why you sleep with me lots."

Monty giggled, squirming as Helen blew raspberries on her cheeks.

Alma turned into her pod, and the others followed. Helen sat on the solid platform with Monty now on her lap.

Finn pressed on. "And what kinds of things does Dartania talk to you about?"

"I don't know." Montana shrugged, like a typical Earth kid would. "Just stuff I guess."

"Why are you worried, Finn? It's not like anyone can get into any trouble or harm." Helen sighed. "Or even any kind of fun here."

"Yeah, you're right. I know." He continued to watch the girl. "It must be the natural fatherly instinct in me."

Helen's head tipped back as laughter erupted from within. She pulled Monty tight to her chest as not to knock the child to the floor. "I'm s-s-s-orry." Her entire face lit up with a rosy glow. "That is just something that I never thought I'd hear you say."

Letting his current probing fall away, Finn moved in on the girls. He planted a soft kiss on Montana's forehead and touched Helen's shoulder, not wanting a repeat fiasco of the other day. He was relieved to have the old Helen back. However that happened, he didn't care to know. "I'm happy to oblige." He knew for sure now that Dartania had said nothing of the opening into the museum, or Monty would have been all over them about it. "I'm going to go to a steam room for a bit."

"Okay," Helen said, her attention still with the girl.

Alma moved toward the door. "I'll come with, if you don't mind?"

"I'd be honored," Finn said with the historical "ladies first" signal, which never lost its appeal.

Once they moved out of hearing distance from the pod, Alma asked, "What has got you all riled up?"

"Let's talk in the steam room." Finn's eyes flicked up to the bodies trailing above, and Alma understood with a nod.

5. Hope

Finnegan and Alma had picked up Paul on their way to the steam room. Now, they sat together while three slugs hovered high above, blurry blobs obscured by the misty air. As they were explaining the new events to Alma, Bertram Grant and Bill Davis entered.

"Ah, perfect timing," Paul said, greeting the men.

Bill flinched back from the big man, staying on the opposite side of the doctor like a beaten dog.

"Look, man." Paul shrugged. "Peace, bro. I am not going to hurt you. I was frustrated. You get it, right?" He looked to the others for validation.

Alma intervened. "Come sit here with me, Bill." She moved slightly to allow the man room to sit between herself and Finnegan.

He accepted her invitation silently by scurrying over and sat hunched between the two.

Alma looked at Paul and kept her voice low. "Let me get this straight. You heard this girl, who has been talking to Monty, say there is a hole into the museum?"

"Technically," Paul said, still pacing, "George Carlisle, Montana's *sperm donor*, overheard the young lady telling Bill here. Which is how we ended up in a scuffle because when I tried to approach him about it, he flipped out."

Bill's face reddened. "I—"

"SHHH!" Everyone else in the room hushed the man as his voice belted out into the oval chamber.

"Oh, sorry, sorry." He lowered his voice to a whisper. "It's just you have to understand. Dartania was only sixteen when we woke up here. She had to go through puberty down here." His round eyes narrowed, the blackened one appearing to be shut completely. Sweat broke out like dew on tips of grass and ran tiny rivers across his face. If it tickled, he drew no attention to it. "She's pretty messed up."

Paul leaned into the circle, entrenching his authority. "Yeah, we've all been through shit down here, Bill. That still doesn't explain why you acted that way."

"Guys, come on." Finnegan glanced up to make sure there were no unusual movements from their captors. So far, all appeared normal. "No matter what transpired before, we need to stick together now."

"It wasn't me I was protecting. It was her," Bill said.

"Bill." Alma drew his attention back. "Perhaps I should talk with her. Actually, I'm quite surprised that I never

[69]

even knew of her." She raised her eyes toward the group. In the mist, the pale grey reflected back almost white, fixating the men's attention. "No one else here has ever heard of her or seen her before? Is that correct?"

The other three men nodded.

"Why did we not know there was a desperate teenager alone here? I am…" She paused, cleared her throat, and resumed. "Excuse me. I was a psychologist on Gaia. Why didn't anyone bring her to me for help? I mean, after all, we have nothing here but to love, guide, and embrace each other."

Bill shifted uncomfortably under everyone gaze. "Don't look at me! She was an angst-ridden kid." He shrugged. "She took off into the women-only area, and even I didn't see her for years."

"I'm sorry, Bill," Alma said easily.

Finnegan cleared his throat. "Now that we all know who Dartania is, can we move on? How are we planning on checking out her claim of an entrance? And if there is, then what?"

"I can go see if she'll talk to me," Alma said.

Paul nodded. "That was the plan."

"Yes, one step at the time. We do not want to awaken their suspicions, if they haven't been already."

Bertram's eyes flicked upward. A new norm in the new life, looking up.

Finn stood, stretching his legs. "Let's break for a few days or a week. Weird how we still talk as though time exists. I have no idea how to reference life now."

Bertram nodded. "It's all we've known. Can't change that now."

"Yeah, I know, you're right… It's just…a reminder of all we've lost." Finn sighed.

"No time to lose hope." Paul slapped Finn on the back. "We're going to get our lives back. His face contorted in a crazy grin.

Bill shuffled to his feet, still wanting to keep a distance from the large man. "Nothing more I can do. Later," he said and exited the steamy cavern.

Alma turned to Finn, addressing his earlier concern on time. "Well, most of us still sleep at the same time. We'll just count sleeps."

Paul nodded.

Bertram shrugged. "What difference does it make? One sleep, ten sleeps, fifty sleeps, we're not going anywhere anytime soon."

"Okay, it's settled. I will go into the women's area and see if I can find Dartania. I'll get her to open up to me, and maybe some of the other women in there know something too. I mean, it's not like they come over here. Funny." Alma paused. "Come to think of it, I've never gone in there either. I don't know why. I suppose it's the same as out here. I just never bothered."

She was more self-reflecting than speaking to the guys, so Bertram made the first move. "Well, there's nothing left much for us to do. Yeah. See you guys in seven sleeps." He got up and left.

The group disbanded, their own personal watch-aliens following them high above on the transparent ceiling.

~~~~~~~

As Alma and Finnegan approached their own area, they heard giggling. Finn shot a look at Alma. "What are those two up to now?"

"I don't know, Finn, but I love the fact that we have Monty here with us. It just wouldn't be the same without her."

Finn agreed. "She keeps us all going."

Rounding the corner, they saw Monty hopping on one foot over piles of their cloth sacks.

"And what's going on here?" he said.

Monty stumbled and spun with a start, and then she saw Finn and Alma and laughed. "Helen is teaching me hopscots."

"Hopscotch? Where did you think of that idea?" Finn said.

"I knew that we couldn't draw on the ground. We have nothing to draw with, and it's like rock." Helen punctuated with a tap of her bare foot. "There's no dust to make lines, so I thought, why not raid the cover-ups? I folded them into little squares and voila."

Alma laughed. "I can't believe we never thought of this before. That's genius, Helen."

"Just another teaching aid for young Monty," Helen said.

"Do you want to join? It's fun. We don't have a rock or a button. Helen says we're supposed to have a rock to toss." The child looked to Helen for confirmation.

"Sort of." Helen waved her to play. "But it's hard to explain. Just keep hopping."

Monty jumped from two spots to one. From two legs to one leg. To the end of the clothes and then back again.

"Plus, it's a good way to get exercise," Helen added.

Watching the girls, Finn's smile couldn't be wider. Even in this moment, aware of where they were, he felt the most at peace just being with the girls. Then, his grin slipped as an errant thought entered his mind. And he wished it hadn't. Back on Gaia, he wanted to have a baby with Helen. He wanted to have a family with Helen. He had envisioned their lives with children on a new planet, building a new world together. Now, none of that would ever be possible.

Monty's sparkling giggle brought him back. He let the old dreams fall from his mind. Regardless, here and now they made him happy, and that was all that mattered.

~~~~~~

After Monty fell asleep, Helen found Alma resting in her cavern. "Fill me in," she said as she sat next to the elderly woman.

"Well, it turns out this Dartania Aswar may have discovered a way into Gaia." At the sound of Helen's gasp, Alma held up a finger in a "wait there's more" gesture. "We don't yet know if this is true or some fantasy made up by a lonely young woman. I suspect she has finally emerged from hiding to find a younger and more interesting person to bond with…"

"Monty."

"Yes, Montana. While there is nothing wrong with that at all, we don't yet know if this person has ulterior motives."

Helen laughed lightly. "Down here…" She opened her arms and swiveled them. "To what end?"

"That is what we must find out, yes?"

"Well, yes of course. We must always protect the child. And what was the big meeting about?"

"It was Paul Smythe who first heard rumor of this, and he's gathered a few people to formulate a plan of escape."

"Escape?" Helen clutched Alma's fingers. "Seriously?"

Alma patted Helen's arm, signaling she was squeezing too tight, and her eyes rolled quickly up and back. "They seem to believe the beings can hear us, or possibly understand us, so they meet in the sauna caves. They think it blocks the vision and they won't suspect a thing. I, however, do not believe they can understand our words, even if they can hear us. What are your thoughts?" Alma probed, knowing full well that Helen had been up with the aliens on a few occasions.

"Oh, umm…" Helen stumbled, unprepared for thoughts of their captors. "No, I don't think they understand our words either. We should be safe to talk."

Alma blatantly stared at the transparent ceiling now, watching the flat wide underside of the two watchers. "I have been watching them, too, you know. They only interfere if we are of any danger to each other or ourselves. It's easy to see. When a person attempts suicide, they gas us, and that person is gone. When a fight breaks out, they gas us to settle the situation. I've observed others not taking their daily supplement and getting thinner and thinner, and then they gas us and said person disappears. My only curiosity is where do they go?" She watched Helen closely with her last statement.

Helen crossed her arms and shivered, even though it was not cold. The temperature never fluctuated, neither too cold nor too hot.

"I try not to worry about that," Helen responded and jumped off the platform. "I'm tired. We'll talk more tomorrow." She gave Alma a quick peck on the cheek and left.

Alma lay back on her firm bed. "Curiouser and curiouser," she quoted from Alice in Wonderland.

~~~~~~

A few sleeps later, Alma made the journey to the women's section. As she walked, she wondered what her personal watcher thought. *Was it curious as to where she was going? Did they have the type of thought pattern that evoked wonderment? Or were they just observers, learning and watching how a different species lives, much as humans used to with insects and animals back on planet Earth?*

Before she realized it, her mental meandering covered the time through the tunnels. Her heart fluttered in her chest. She felt a bit out of place and was taken aback by her own trepidation.

"Come on, Alma, nothing's going to bite you. After all, every one of these people were on Gaia too." She ducked through the narrow opening, stopped briefly to quench her dismay, and pushed on.

As she passed by large open caverns, all heads turned. The ladies' mouths opened. They stopped talking, blinked in surprise, and watched her go by. Alma looked at the women with a slight smile in her eyes, letting them know that she was just passing through. Monty was right; this place was larger than their area. The women banded together in groups, and it had a different vibe. She couldn't yet explain the vibe, but she wasn't sure she liked it.

A voice rang out behind her and as she paused, more joined in.

"Who are you?"

"What do you want here?"

"Ya, what do you want?"

Alma turned to face the women. "Hi, my name is Alma Klein." She didn't recognize any of the faces in the small crowd, but it had been years since the ship had crashed. "I am looking for a young woman named Dartania."

The apparent leader of the group, a tall woman with short, flat, tawny hair and eerie white eyes like a husky, took two steps closer. "What do you want her for?"

"Just to talk to her. She has been coming out to the mixed area of late. I heard Bill Davis is her uncle and her parents died in the crash." Alma spoke honestly, thinking a half-truth would gain her more ground than a lie.

"Yeah, so." The tall woman's face contorted in genuine anger. "What does all that mean to you? We've never seen you before."

Alma held up her hands in supplication. "I was the psychologist on Gaia, and as I said, I am only learning of Dartania. I thought perhaps I can be a good sounding board for her."

The tall woman's jaw visibly clenched. "She's got us already. Go." She turned, pointing to the way out, the crowd shuffling back to clear a passageway. It was clear this woman was in charge and not about to let a stranger in.

"Okay, easy." Alma walked toward the group. She kept her head high but did not make eye contact with the tall woman. As she passed by the others, she said quietly to anyone that wanted to listen. "Tell her I'm with Monty if she wants to talk." Then she was beyond the group and headed back the way she came. She heard them following her until she reached the opening out. She did not bother to glance back, just kept moving farther and farther away.

~~~~~

Finnegan spotted Alma as she walked past Paul's cubby-hole, where the men were talking. "Alma." He rushed out, stopping the older woman.

"Oh, Finn, Paul. Sorry, I was lost in thought."

"Any news? Did you find the girl?"

"No." She saw Finn's face drop. "I'll either need to wait and watch for her to come see Montana again, or I will have to send Monty in to bring Dartania out. They are very protective in there, and even though I am a woman, they don't trust me."

Finn waited as two people passed by them in the corridor before speaking in a hushed tone. "The question is how much do we tell Monty? If she thinks there is adventure around the corner, you know darn well she'll be off searching and draw attention."

"No. You are correct there. She is a child." Alma pondered the situation and said, "Well, we could just tell her we want to meet her new friend and see how that plays out…or as I said, wait for the girl to come to us."

Paul crossed his arms. "All we do is wait. We've been waiting for years. Let's get this party started. Send the kid in."

More people walked by and glanced at the group as Paul's voice carried through the passage.

"You're the psychologist. What do you think?" Finn said to Alma.

"Won't hurt to try."

"You all sort that out. I'm going to sleep." With that said, Paul ducked back into his chamber and stretched out on his platform.

Finnegan and Alma walked back to their own pods, discussing what they should tell Monty.

Not long after, they came upon Helen teaching the child basic math using only her fingers. Monty was fidgety, obviously bored with the lessons and was happy when she saw Finnegan approaching. "Finn!" She bounced to her feet. "Can we go back to the pictures again today? I want to see the colors again."

"Sure, why not." He smiled down at her.

"Let's all go together," Alma suggested.

Montana liked that idea even better. She bounced on the balls of her feet and turned to race off, but Alma stopped her. "Walk with us, okay?" She restrained the girl by the shoulder.

Helen, however, begged out of the trip. "You know what? I'm not in the mood for the museum today. I'm going to go lay down."

"Oh…" Alma started to respond to Helen's statement, but noticed Monty's wrinkled brow and acted like nothing was amiss. "Have a nice nap," she called out.

The three headed off toward the museum once again.

Finnegan had seen Alma's response and made a mental note to ask her about it as soon as Monty was not around. For now, they needed to deal with Monty and Dartania. As they walked, Alma talked about various things, and she slipped smoothly into her psychologist hat. "You know, I would really like to meet your new friend. Dartania, is it?"

This got Monty excited again. She bounced, her curls floating about her head. "I knew it. I told her to come say hi to you all last time she was over. But she got scared and ran away. Why would she be scared? Everyone here takes good care of me." Monty paused, her bounce slowing. "Except for George. He doesn't help." That sent her off on a new trajectory. "Why doesn't George help take care of me, Alma?"

"Some people don't know how to talk to children, is all," Alma stated matter-of-factly.

Monty's delicate laugh tinkled through the solemn tunnels. "That's silly. He can talk to me like you do. I understand English, you know."

"Why of course you do, sweetie." Alma didn't want to get into a conversation about Monty's father at the moment, but she saw that the child was hurting, it would be something they would have to circle back to. "As for your friend, I think because she has been in with the women for so long that she's just scared of the boys. Maybe you can take me in there, to her place? I think she would meet me where it is safe."

They arrived at the art gallery, and Monty tore away from Alma. As she ran off to her favorite painting, she called back, "Sure, let's do that."

Finn had kept silent the whole time and now said to Alma, "Good job." Then he heard the hiss of gas coming and looked up. "What the hell?" He took a few steps toward Monty and passed out.

6. Helen

Cries of pain echoed through the corridor. Finnegan ran hard and fast. His bare feet were slapping the rock floor with a resounding smack, and he knew they were going to hurt later. He couldn't care about that now. He needed to help the screamer. As he closed in on the sound, his heart sank; he knew it was Wendy giving birth. There was no stopping nature. There was not much hope for her or the baby in their new surroundings. Finn knew this, the mother knew it too. They all did. But they would make the best of it, and work together to help her.

Wendy was laid out on the softest bed they could create for her, a mass of their new potato sacks. Someone had clearly been prepared, or perhaps she always had the softest bed in the colony—what did he know? He moved into the chamber with Dr. Grant Bertram, Alma Klein, and Wendy and George Carlisle. Finn was surprised that the father was there, for he'd noticed that the man avoided Wendy as much as he possibly could, given their space.

Wendy's shrill screams of pain were deafening inside the chamber. Blood pooled on the fabric. It covered the lower half of her body and Dr. Bertram's arms and hands. "Push harder, Wendy. You can do it."

Alma sat cradling Wendy's head in her lap. "It's okay, honey, your baby is coming. You'll hold her soon enough."

Wendy grabbed Alma's arm, her eyes rimmed red against a pallid grey face, and Finn saw at that moment that the woman was going to die. "Promise me…" Her eyes closed, and her teeth clenched, he muscles in her jaw frozen in atrophy. Then her mouth opened, and no more screams came.

Dr. Bertram slipped the baby into his arms. "It's a girl." He held her up for momma to see, and the smile slipped from his face. He immediately got back to work helping the motherless newborn.

George's face paled near that of the dead woman's. He pushed past Finn, not saying a word. He just ran off.

Finn moved to Alma's side and helped her out from under Wendy's heavy head. He pulled one of the sacks from beneath her and covered her now peaceful face. "What did she ask you?"

"To take care of the baby and name her Montana after her home on Earth."

The image of Dr. Bertram and Montana, the newborn, slipped back into darkness as Finnegan began to wake.

He blinked away the memory and the pain of that day as the seven years without life returned to his consciousness. Sitting up, he shook away the cobwebs.

"What now?" he asked no one and moved from his platform to find the others once again.

Finn checked on Montana first, and she was still sleeping. He went to Helen's pod and found it empty. He ran into Alma as she was leaving her space. "Is Helen with you?"

A shadow fell across Alma's fair features, and she tried to pull out of it, but Finn noticed. "What has been bothering you?" he asked, his voice tight and low.

Alma looked around and, seeing others walking toward them, pulled Finnegan into her chamber. "I think they took her again," she said.

Finn sputtered. "Wha…took her… What do you mean 'took her again'?"

"Finn, hear me out please." Alma held up her hands in an effort to calm the man before she could even begin. "Helen has gone and been returned before. I think four times, but I am not sure."

Finn was taken aback. He felt betrayed. His mind raced. Down here, all they had left was each other. How could she do this to him? How could she not tell him this? Helen was his everything, his world, the last of his world. He stumbled for a moment, started to say something, and then changed his mind.

Alma said, "I do understand, Finn. I...trust me, I know what you're going through. I didn't know what to think. I wanted to observe her. I wanted to see if there was any change in her, other than she would get really depressed, and then come back normal again, and she didn't seem to notice that there was a difference. She didn't remember being suicidal, Finn. Remember when was she suicidal?" Alma lowered her head. "I never told you because I never wanted to worry you. I know that there is nothing for you, other than her and Monty."

"And you," he said. "I just don't want there to be secrets. Hell, down here, I never expected there to be secrets."

"I understand that. I don't want there to be secrets either, Finn. I just was trying to understand what was happening and not freak her out. What do you think she would do if she knew that she had been taken up with the aliens? How would she handle that? What would she think?" Alma pleaded her case.

He said, "How do we handle that? What do we think?"

"Honestly, I believe that they are helping her. I don't know where the others go; none of us do. Do we? Do they kill our people? Do they shoot them out into space? Are they up there like guinea pigs, being poked and prodded and who knows what else? Or…" She held up a finger, and the corners of her lips peeked up. "Are they the blessed ones and put out of their misery? Allowed to rest? It's all questions, Finn. Helen doesn't know. She doesn't remember going. You saw how she was the last time. I mean you tried to kiss her, and she lost her mind. She screamed like a mad woman, and the next thing you know, poof she's gone. Then, suddenly she's back, and she's happy and normal. Back to the way that she was before this. I'm sorry I had to pretend I didn't know that."

Seeing the still-hurt look on Finnegan's face, she took his chin in her papery soft finger and tilted his eyes to hers. "I'm truly sorry that I hid that from you. I do think that she does something for them that none of us can do. I believe they need her alive and happy. They take her when she gets sad, and they make her better. She helps them, and they help her in return. I don't think they are bad beings, Finn. I don't even know they have emotions the same way we do, but I don't think they are trying to hurt us either."

Finn raised his head to the ceiling, flabbergasted. "Not hurt us? Do you not think this doesn't hurt us?" He raised his arms to the ceiling. "Look around you. We have nothing. We are no longer humans. We're what…ants in a fucking colony of people. I don't even know what to say. This is not life, Alma. This is not life."

"I know it's not, but do they know that? If this is their way of life, then who's to say? What are the alternatives? That is what we now might have the opportunity to find out."

"Okay." Finn sighed, knowing to fight was pointless and might get them gassed again. "You've been observing. What have you observed?"

"As I said, I really think that they are not here to hurt us, and somehow they use Helen to help them. We have to figure out what that help is. Truth be told…" She paused, keeping her gaze directly on Finn. "We know there is no possible way that Gaia can fly out of here. I mean how many miles underground are we? The ship is in a million pieces, spread out here and there—and locked away in a museum. I don't know what Paul's grand scheme is, but I think we just need to forget about the ship and get to the surface."

"The surface." Finn chuffed. "We're on an alien planet as goddamn keepsakes. We need a way out."

"Clearly, Paul did not have a solid plan, and you were on his side. I'm at a loss too. We're going to have to get everyone together and come up with a better plan of action. That ship will not help us."

A movement caught his eye, and Finn looked up in time to see Tattoo sliding away. "Uh, you realize we just discussed this outside of a safe room."

"Why do you assume anywhere is safe? Or that they can even understand what we are saying?" Alma's head tilted, studying the man's face.

"Another mystery, isn't it, Alma? Where do you think tattoo-butt is going? In all my time awake, I've never seen it leave me." He pointed up.

"Yes, Finn, another mystery."

"Goodnight, Alma. We'll talk tomorrow."

~~~~~

Finn awoke after presumably seven to eight hours of sleep and went straight off to Helen's chamber. His heart dropped when he saw it was still empty. Trying to stay positive, he went next to Alma's, and her spot was also empty. "Oh for two," he mumbled and went to check on Montana. But she, too, was gone. He checked the museum and asked a few wanderers. No one had seen any of the ladies. As much as he hated to do it, he went to George. The man was sitting on his platform, picking at a toenail.

"George," Finn called out for the man's attention.

George dropped his stubby foot and looked up. "What?"

"Have you seen Monty, Alma, or Helen today?"

"Geeze, you never let up do you?"

"I never give up. There's a difference, George. And if you want to be in on this plan, then you'd better get with the program."

"Why, you got new news?" The man's beady eyes narrowed to slits.

Finnegan waved him off. Clearly, the man knew nothing. "Only that Monty was going to take Alma into the women's area to find Dartania. That's probably where they went, so it'll be a while anyway."

As Finn began walking away, George yelled out his doorway, "Be sure to keep me in the loop!"

Finnegan held back the urge to give the man the finger and wandered off to find someone decent to talk to.

Passing pod after pod, some with people talking, others empty or a single soul sitting quietly, Finn was feeling depressed. He realized that up until this business of a way out had been brought to his attention, he had gotten complacent with the new way of life. He had a routine of sorts. Now he was restless again, just like when they first awoke here. He was anxious for some action, some physical activity, perhaps even a full-fledged war. He stopped short and took two steps back, blinking. Much to his surprise, Bill Davis, Bertram Grant, Preston Haywood, and Russell Emerson were sitting in a row, listening to Pastor Carl Mayweather's sermon.

Finnegan eased into the room, walked the outer edge of the seated people, and sat beside Preston. He looked down the line of men as they turned to the disturbance. He shrugged at them, trying to convey his confusion.

Preston leaned close and whispered, "Just listen."

While not one for religion, and he hadn't thought the others were either, Finn gave them the benefit of doubt and listened as Pastor Mayweather spoke.

"...and that person among us shall be our Savior, as Christ, our Lord Jesus, returned to save us. History does repeat itself, regardless of what planet we may reside. The Lord does not look away because we are not on Earth. For the Lord created everything. He created time, space, matter—yes, matter. You and I and even dare I say it..." He paused, his wide-set eyes challenging the group to deny him his speech. He raised a finger skyward, and all eyes followed the path to the transparent ceiling. It was covered, nearly a solid mass, of alien beings. As every person in the group had a follower, even Finn's own Tattoo was back. Hushed voices murmured through the crowd, then a loud clap brought them back to the pastor. "That's right, folks. He even created the creatures here and now. He has a reason for this. He has a purpose for everything. We have to ask ourselves..." Mayweather's voice dipped to a whisper. He had everyone leaning in to his words. "What did we do to be placed here?"

Finnegan had enough. Sure, the man's voice was as calming as a babbling brook over sand-washed pebbles, but his words were still gobbledygook as far as he was concerned. He waited for the pastor's voice to resume a normal tone, and then he slipped back out the way he came. He headed down toward the women's entrance to wait for Alma and Monty to return.

~~~~~

Monty led Alma through the tunnels of the women's area, as though she had traversed them many times. When in reality, she had only been in there twice, or so she'd said. Once again, Alma was wowed by the size of their caverns. They were deeper, wider, and had taller ceilings than those back in the common area, and she wondered how they came to take over this space without any confrontation from the others. Thinking back to the early days, she couldn't even recall any type of stand-off happening and wondered why. Monty stopped abruptly in front of her, jarring her memeory. *Yes,* she thought, at that time she had been taking care of an enormously pregnant and terrified Wendy. "Is something wrong?"

Monty pointed into a steam room. It was similar to the ones in their own area, except that there was a pile of sacks outside the door. Even through the steam, you could see the naked ladies leaning against the walls. Some were talking, some resting, and one with long black hair sat in the center with her back to the entrance.

"Is that her?" Alma whispered.

"Ya, I think it is."

"Okay, well we shouldn't disturb the ladies' resting time." She tapped Monty on the shoulder, who never having seen people naked before was naturally curious and staring. "Take me all the way to her pod."

"How come they have their dresses off?" Monty asked as she turned and continued down the corridor.

"It's freeing to be naked." As she said it, Alma realized she hadn't been completely nude in years and suddenly had the urge to go join the ladies in a hot steam. "See, in our area, we have men and women together, and our bodies look different. Therefore, we keep our dresses on for…privacy… Over here, the ladies' bodies are all the same, and they can be without their sacks and still feel safe."

"Well, not all their bodies looked the same to me," Monty said.

"Yes, you're right, we are all a bit different." Alma was going to say "like snowflakes" but then realized she'd have to explain snowflakes, and that would open an entirely new subject. She tried to simplify it. "See my hand?" She held out her hand. "And your hand?" Monty held hers up beside Alma's. "Mine is a different size and color, and I have wrinkles. Your hand is small and pink and young. It is that way with every person; we are all a bit different. But men and woman are different in other ways, ways that make us uncomfortable to be naked around each other."

"Okay." Monty shrugged, bored of the topic, and turned into a chamber that must've been Dartania's sleeping area.

Alma sighed, noting that although it may never be an issue, they should have the sex talk with the child. She looked about the space. Of course, it was like everyone else's, except that her area was filled with the potato sack outfits. There were piles stacked neatly around the entire room. They were at least four feet high and two piles deep, with a few piles reaching the transparent ceiling. They were folded to marine standards, neat, tight, and wrinkle-free. The only place where they were messy was on her platform. She had made herself a cozy spot with mounds of balled-up sacks. It looked as if a person could disappear into the bed and be totally camouflaged.

Monty laughed and jumped up onto the bed. "How come we don't do this? It's so soft," she purred as she snuggled into the makeshift bedding.

Alma was at a loss for words. *Why did they never think to use the dresses as blankets or pillows?* "Huh" was all she managed. Then a voice from behind brought her attention back, and she spun to find a beautiful, fresh-faced young woman standing behind her. Her long black hair shimmered with dew, her eye's large and calf-like, unblinking, stoic.

"This is my room," Dartania stated, stepping beyond Alma with her arms crossed.

Alma tapped her chest, as though speaking to some who didn't speak English. "Hi, my name is Alma, and I believe you know Montana."

The young woman didn't acknowledge the greeting. Her head tilted slightly, and her lips turned down. "This is my room," she repeated.

"HEY," a loud voice rang over Alma's head, causing her flinch. "What are you doing in here?"

Alma spun again, this time to face the tall woman from her first trip into the women's area. "Hi, my na—"

"I don't care what your name is." The tall woman with the creepy white eyes stepped closer, hovering threateningly above Alma. "I thought I told you not to come here. Now get your brat and get out."

Monty cringed under the pile of dresses. She never faced a person's anger like this in her short years. Sweat broke out on her brow, and she wanted nothing more than to hide.

"Come on, Monty." Alma motioned her over, and the girl flew to her side, clutching at her leg. "Clearly, we are not wanted here. Although, I don't know why. We are, after all, women too," she said snidely, keeping her head high for she had nothing to fear.

The tall woman slid back enough to allow the interlopers to pass and then closed the gap by moving into the doorway as they exited. "I mean it. Don't let me catch you here again."

This time it was Alma who led them out of the women's area. As others gathered in doorways to watch, Monty said, "I don't think I like it here after all."

"Me neither, kid, me neither."

~~~~~

As soon as the ladies appeared in the tunnel of the common area, Finnegan was on them. "Well, did you find her? Did you talk to her?"

"We should talk about this later, Finn," Alma said with a glance down at Monty.

Finn understood. He'd let the excitement get the better of him and had not given thought to the child. "Of course. I'm sorry."

"There was a mean lady in there! And they had no clothes on, Finn."

"A mean lady?" he asked.

Alma nodded. "Yes, their leader that I told you about appeared again, and she is not keen on outsiders. Even of the female persuasion."

"Okay, and no clothes? I have to know."

"They sauna naked." Alma sighed. "Wouldn't that be a treat, Finn?"

"Uh, I suppose." It wasn't something he ever thought about. Being of the hunter mind, clothes were always essential.

"Let's go back to our area and check for you-know-who, and we can talk later."

Alma nodded. She was curious to know if Helen was back yet. If not, this would be the longest time span without her, and they would have to tell Montana something.

Once they were back in their own comfort zone, Monty took off running. Finnegan let her, as this allowed him to speak freely. "What's the deal back there?"

"It's going to be tougher than you think, Finn. I saw Dartania, and even though she only spoke two words to me…" She paused, wanting to be sure what she was about to say held truth. But she was 95 percent sure, and if she was wrong, it wouldn't matter. "I believe she has Asperger's syndrome."

"I've heard the term before, but I'm not exactly sure what that means. How is it going to affect us?"

Alma took a breath and explained, "The symptoms vary from person to person, but the basics are, limited or inappropriate social interactions, robotic or repetitive speech, above average verbal skills, tendency to discuss self rather than others, awkward movements and or mannerisms… Well, and the list goes on—"

Finn interrupted, "And you know she has this from two words?"

"Technically it was four words, 'This is my room,' but it was how she said it, the way she carried herself, the expression on her face, and the fact that she had stacks upon stacks of our sack dresses in her room. There are many *tells* when you know what you are seeing." Alma slowed her pace as they were nearing their area, and Monty could be around any corner. "As for the second part of your question. This can be detrimental to your plans because if she doesn't want to share her knowledge, she won't. Simple as that."

Finn stopped and took Alma's arm, forcing her to face him. "But she came here looking for Montana. She wanted Monty to go live there with her. Why? After all these years, why?"

Alma's grey gaze softened as a small smile found her mouth. "I think she's lonely for someone younger and freer. I'm sure she'd heard talk of the child and was just looking for a friend. First, you need to sort things out with the camp counselor. Find out who the tall woman is and why she won't allow anyone in. Then, we'll worry about Dartania."

Finn blinked, feeling defeated for the first time in years as Alma turned and walked away. Then the thought of Helen came back to the forefront, and he let the rest go. One problem at a time.

7. Now What

For some, a few more sleeps had passed, but not Finnegan. He barely slept at all. Helen was gone for good this time, and they did not know why. She had been back to her old self, happy and playing with Montana. And next, poof—gone. He and Alma had sat down with Monty and explained as best they could, that they really knew nothing, and Helen was gone.

The questions came. *Will she be back—we don't know. Where did she go—we don't know. Why did they take her—we don't know. Monty ran off crying. "You know nothing!" she'd screamed at them.* Neither were sure they'd ever seen her cry before. Sometimes she would get bored or frustrated with their situation, but she was never sad or scared—until the day in the women's area with the tall lady yelling. And that night when Alma went to check on her, Monty had her platform over-spilling with the sack dresses. She was all huddled up in the pile with a mournful pout across her face. Since that day, she had refused to talk or go to the museum.

Finnegan, being the man he was and not knowing children before Montana, headed off to talk with the men about the new developments.

He tracked down Bill Davis and Bertram Grant, who went off and found Paul Smythe, Russell Emerson, and Preston Haywood. They all gathered back in the steam room, same as before.

Finnegan looked about the tight space as all the men gathered around in a circle. "Do we really need to have this many people every time?"

"Be thankful George isn't here," Paul said.

"Hey, we need to know what's happening too," Preston added.

Finn squinted at the man through the steam. "We are trying to sort out how to get into the women's area. How is an astronomer going to help with that?"

"For starters, I'm a fucking genius." Preston defended. "You—"

"Fellows!" Bertram called for attention. "We're all here to help. Whether it's at this meeting or another one, it's best if we attend as many as possible to stay in the loop."

Russell nodded along, saying nothing.

Bill shook his head, his hair as always doing a comical floating wave about his visible scalp. "Finn? Why didn't you stay for the sermon the other day? You have to listen to what Pastor Carl is talking about."

"Yeah." A few voices mixed as one.

Finn was taken aback. "What does some God spouting sermon have to do with this situation?"

Russell broke in and said, "Oh, you have to hear it from the beginning, Finnegan. He's predicting our future."

"What?" Finn couldn't believe what he was hearing—and from Russell Emerson, the famed pilot of Gaia. "Have you all gone mad?"

Paul cocked his head. "What's this about a sermon? No one said anything to me. And I agree with Finn—have you gone mad? Maybe we don't need you after all." He bared his teeth to the men sitting around him.

"No, no." Bill slapped his exposed knees. "It's true. You have to hear it all the way through. It's kind of in Bible-speak, but I think he's doing it on purpose to confuse the slugs. He talks of our savior, a way out of the caves, the surface, the slugs…" He inhaled a quick breath. "Just go one day."

Finn shook his head. "Okay, enough of this for now. We need to discuss what Alma found in the women's area."

"Yes, what did Alma find in the women's area? Do tell," a female voice rang out from the entrance to the sauna, startling the men.

"Ah geez, Brenda, what are you doing here?" Paul bellowed.

Brenda Kelly placed a pudgy finger to her oversized lips. "Shhh, or you know who will gas us again." She pointed upward then moved in, uninvited and unwelcome, and sat directly between Finnegan and Bill. "Sooo… What're all the secret meetings about?"

Finn had to physically withhold a shudder as her shoulder rubbed up against him. He shuffled a foot left so they wouldn't be touching. "Why are you here, Brenda?"

She tilted her head toward him and batted her eyelashes. "Is there something better I should be doing?"

"Never mind." Paul waved her off and said, "Go on, Finn. What happened?"

Finnegan wasn't thrilled about talking in front of Brenda, but clearly no one else cared, so he told them about the encounter between Alma and the woman. He finished up, turning to Bill. "Did you know that Dartania has Asperger's?"

Bill shook his head. "Not that I was aware of. I mean, she was always different, but I just thought it was the way she was raised. You know, at her age being taken away from Earth, living on the ship, then losing her parents. I just figured it all messed with her head."

"Well, Alma seems to believe otherwise," Finn said.

Paul cleared his throat, drawing everyone's attention. "Brenda, you worked in the kitchen on Gaia. Do you know a really tall lady that was ornery?"

"Hmm, tall mean lady… Well, the tallest woman I knew was Linda Walker, but I can't say she was nasty in any way."

"This place changes people," Bertram said.

"Hey, I knew a Linda," Russell added, "and I haven't seen her since we crashed. I assumed she was dead, but it's probably her. She was a wellness guru back in the day and one tough cookie."

"Okay, now we're getting somewhere. And luckily with Brenda crashing in on us, maybe she can be of service?" Paul stated.

Brenda rubbed her palms on her exposed knees. Finn caught the motion out of the corner off his eye and was glad he was not sitting directly across from her, as her dress was pulled taut across her thighs and most likely exposing her. She said, "Yes, anything to do in this godforsaken place! Fill me in, what's going on?"

Paul told Brenda everything, about Dartania coming to Monty, that there may or may not be a hole into the museum, and that they were being blocked—or cock-blocked, as he so eloquently put it—by the Amazon, Linda.

"Oh-oh! This is exciting, isn't it," Brenda said. "All these years, and we may finally have a way out?"

"Yes, but we're taking it slow, Brenda," Finn said. "We don't want them to get suspicious and figure out we're up to something. Who knows what they'll do... Oh..." He paused for a second and resumed speaking. "I guess I should tell you all that with our last gassing, they took Helen."

"WHAT!" the group echoed together, then the questions began to fly.

"Look, we don't know, right? Alma thinks they need her to help with something." Finn sighed. It was now or never. "Apparently, this is not the first time they have taken her. There have been others. But they always returned her quickly, and she was happier after. Alma's been watching her."

Paul stood quickly and began pacing. "Finnegan, why didn't she tell us? What, she's a spy for them?"

Bill broke in and said, "Ya, what if they implanted her with a listening device?"

"Calm down." Finn stood, too, not wanting to feel overpowered by Paul's lumbering form. "I'm sure it's nothing to do with us or this."

"You'd better be right." Paul jabbed a finger at him.

Brenda stood, too, intercepting the men. "Guys, please. If you get too hyper, they will gas us. Calm down. I will go talk to Alma and come up with a plan of action to get past Linda…or get Linda on our side. Whatever we need to do to get out of here."

Preston, who had been a silent observer for most the conversation, finally stood too. "Maybe we need to think bigger. Why not tell everyone, and then instead of running into stumbling blocks and tripping over each other, we can actually work together."

Paul's smile took over his face as he clapped Preston's boney back. "Always the voice of reason, eh, Presto! However, we have to make sure this hole exists before we get everyone's hopes up. Then, we can talk about spreading the news. I mean, we are going to have to get men into the women's area somehow. What better way than to have them on board." He clapped loudly in the echoing chamber.

"Okay, let's start with Brenda and Alma. We'll meet back here in four sleeps?" He looked at everyone to be sure they were on the same page. "Yes, let's do this."

~~~~~

Finnegan was turning the corner toward the museum when Alma waved him over to her pod. "Monty was asking for you."

"How's she doing?"

"Well, she stayed buried all day today, but then when I tried to peek in on her, she asked for you. It looked like she'd been crying."

Finn shook his head. "Can't say I blame her. Sometimes I wish I could cry."

Alma's brow raised, but she kept quiet. She turned back the way they had come as they reached Montana's room and Finn entered.

"Hey, I hear someone is looking for me?" He poked at the pile of sacks, pretending he couldn't see her through the mess, though she was a giant hump in the center.

Suddenly, a bunch of the material scattered to the floor as she sat upright. Her jade-green eyes, usually vibrant and full of laughter, were clouded with pain and rimmed red. Her cheeks were a rosy tomato color from all the crying.

Finn's heart tugged at the sight. He never thought there'd be a day he'd see the sweet little girl downtrodden.

"Tell me a story about Earth, Finn. A happy fun story, 'kay?"

"Hmm, let me see." He tapped his chin, thinking of a good tale to cheer up the child. "How about you scoot over there and let me sit on your comfy new bed."

Monty shuffled the pile of cloth around, swung her legs over the edge of the platform, and waited for Finnegan to get comfortable. Once he did, she snuggled up under his arm, like a baby bird tucking under momma's wing, and her thumb went into her mouth.

Finn was shocked by that; he'd never seen her do that before. But he ignored it and went ahead with a tale he thought she might like. "Did I ever tell you about the day I saw a rabbit save a bear's life?" he asked.

Monty made a noise that he took as no, so he began. "It was a perfect autumn day, one of those days where the wind has a crisp freshness to it and you can smell the snow in the air. Though you know it's not quite there yet, as the sun peeks in and out of high white clouds. The mountaintops off in the distance always hold frosted peeks, and before long, the entire land will be a blanket of pureness. The leaves have all fallen off the trees, and they whirl and rustle into the wind and under my feet. It's a great day to walk through the woods and enjoy the last days of fall. I know my way around these trails like the back of my hand. I am walking quietly, listening to the forest around me. You always have to be aware of your surroundings." He teaches as he tells the story. "The birds are singing to each other before the long cold comes. Squirrels are scampering around the mossy floor, foraging for nuts. When off in the distance, I hear a great roar. I dodge this way and that, ducking from tree to tree. I know it's a bear, a big bear. And when I get close enough, I see that it is a big black bear. He's well over fifteen feet tall, almost as tall as the trees around me. He is attacking a dead tree stump with all his might! He's digging and snuffling. The bark is flying. His face is covered in fresh honey and bees!"

Monty laughs as Finn shakes his head, slaps at his cheeks, and makes roaring noises along with this tale.

"The food he found was not yet abandoned. He had disturbed a beehive. They were all over him, stinging his snout and his eyes. He was getting madder and madder by the second. He roared again and lifted himself onto his hind legs. Next, he turned in a circle and took four huge steps out of the clearing and right onto the path of a steel-jawed bear trap." Finn hopped off the platform and lumbered around the space, his arms raised over his head like an angry bear, stomping and roaring.

Monty gasped when she heard the words "bear trap," as Finn had spent much time explaining hunting and how life worked on Earth.

"Just as his front paw was about to come crashing down and land directly into the trap, a jackrabbit came out of nowhere, bouncing right at the bear." He crouched down and pounced toward Monty, getting more giggles. "Well, the black bear was startled by the sudden movement in front of him. Still angry from the bee stings, he reared back up and roared in anger. Then he turned the other way, moving safely from the rabbit and the trap. The rabbit bebopped along, not even stopping to be afraid of the bear. And that is how the rabbit saved a bear from getting hurt in a trap."

"That was a good story." Monty squinted, her freckled nose wrinkling up. "Is it true, Finn? Did that actually happen to you and the bear?"

"Yes, it really did happen. Funny things happen in life all the time. We just have to keep our eyes open and watch for them."

She squirmed in the pile on her platform. "But funny things don't happen here, do they, Finn?" Her voice mellowed and drawn again.

Finnegan placed his arm across her tiny shoulders and made a decision without consulting the group. "Things might be changing here, too, Monty."

She peered under her eyelids at him, ready for adventure but still upset. "How?"

"Can I trust you with the biggest secret you've ever heard in your entire life?"

That got her attention. She bounced up onto her knees, her jade-green eyes once again vibrant with color. "YES!"

"Okay." He hesitated now, not sure if he was doing the right thing, but he desperately wanted her to be happy. "We heard that your new friend, Dartania, might have found a way into the museum."

Monty's arms flew up, tossing the sacks into the air with the sudden movement, and yelped loudly.

Finn jumped back and then reached out to brace Monty by the shoulders. "Shhh!" He stopped her from bouncing and pointed up at the two watchers above. "You don't want them to think something is wrong."

Monty laughed and waved at the clear ceiling. "Hi, slugies, everything is great." She continued to laugh.

Finn rubbed his face, mumbling, "Oh, geez," and then said aloud to Monty, "But we have to be calm. We have to wait until an adult can talk with Dartania and get more information. You must promise me you'll relax."

She stopped bouncing around and kneeled up close to Finn again. "Can we go in and see the art?"

"When and if we can get in, yes, I will take you to see the art up close." He smiled, knowing that telling her was the right thing. It would take her mind off the missing Helen, and now perhaps they could enlist her help with Dartania.

Monty yawned. "I'm sleepy now. I'm going to sleep first, okay?"

Finnegan knew that this day, filled with tears and then unsurmountable excitement, was a greater day than she had yet experimented in her short, dull life. "You've gotten some pretty exciting news, and it's worn you out. You rest, and I'll check on you later." He kissed her warm forehead as she nestled down into her new makeshift bed. As he walked away, he sighed. Now he'd have to let everyone know that he told the child.

It didn't matter. Things were changing, and for better or worse, it was the one thing they all needed the most.

~~~~

"What's the matter, you can't keep up with a girl?" Helen glided on one foot, her arms held out to her sides and her hair flying up behind her.

Finn pushed harder with his back skate to gather some speed. "Take off the skates, and I'll pass you."

Helen spun in an elegant pirouette. She tilted her head, crossed her arms, and turned into an invisible warp of colors. As she slowed, Finn approached, admiring her rosy-red cheeks, and he grabbed her waist as he passed and pulled her into his arms. Her cold lips pressed into his. Together they spun off on long lazy circles.

"I love you, Helen Corman."

"I love you, too, Finnegan Brennan."

Nestling into her coconut-smelling hair, he said, "How do you feel about Helen Brennan?"

"Well, I've never met her before. Would I like her?" Her laughter carried through the ice dome as she pushed away and skated off again.

As Finn raised his gaze toward the star-spangled ceiling, his vision began to fade, the icy coolness of the room warmed, and with a blink, he was back underground in his pod. "I wish we died, Helen." He rubbed his face and sat up. "I truly do."

Then, a thought popped into his head. He, only this second, realized that he had not seen Mark Jones since his first trip to the women's area to find Montana.

With renewed purpose, he hopped off his platform and out into the tunnels. He knew Mark's pod was in the next section on the opposite side of the museum. He passed the art gallery, the wardrobe room, the kitchen, the showers, and slid around the corner from the library and into the next area.

As a couple approached, he asked, "Have you seen Mark Jones?"

They glanced at each other, frowning and shaking their heads, but kept on unconcerned. Everyone that passed by, he questioned. No one had seen him, and no one cared. Finn turned into what he hoped was Mark's sleeping area; they were all identical. There was no one in it and nothing of interest to see. Finn spun around. "Do people not care at all anymore?" he called into the space then hung his head, took a deep breath, and moved back the way he came.

As he continued on, he saw the pastor Carl Mayweather coming toward him. "Hey, can I talk to you?" Finn asked.

The pastor stopped. "Anytime. What can I do for you?" His voice was as smooth as before, but Finn found his wide-set, dark eyes unsettling.

"Listen, some of the men are saying that your sermons are..." Finn chuckled, he couldn't believe he was saying this out loud. "Predictions of the future." He tried to relax his face from the disdain he could feel tightening it.

"You have not then listened to one of my sermons?"

"No." Finn didn't play games.

"Well." The pastor crossed his arms and cupped his elbows, and with a slight nod, he said, "You should. They are, if I dare say, enlightening."

Finn felt heat raising to face. "Did you know that they took Helen Corman? Did you know that? Could you stop that?"

The pastor didn't blink an eye. "Genesis two fifteen; the Lord God took the man and put him into the garden of Eden to cultivate it and keep it." He turned away, and as he was walking, called back, "Come to my sermon."

"What is that supposed to mean?" Finn yelled down the corridor, throwing up his hands. "What do you mean!"

Frustrated that the pastor was of no help, Finn continued to on to Paul's. Seeing him in his space, he turned in without announcing himself, startling the big man. "Have you noticed Mark Jones around lately?"

"Shit, Finn! A man could still have a heart attack, you know."

"Sorry. I just had a weird encounter with Mayweather."

"The pastor? What happened?"

"I confronted him about his prediction sermons, or whatever they are, and he gave me some mumbo jumbo about the garden of Eden and man cultivating it and—" Finn stopped talking. His eyes widened, and he looked to Paul. "Wait a minute. Mark Jones was a botanist, and so was Helen. Shit, if he's been missing for weeks now, and Helen is gone, do you think…"

Paul caught the excitement and let out a loud whoop, it echoed deafeningly through his chamber and out into the tunnels. "Maybe we have vegetation upstairs! Whoooo!" He leaned back, fist clenched, and howled at the ceiling then turned and scooped Finnegan up into his arms.

"Hey, stop it!" Finn slapped the big man on the back in effort to be put back to the ground. As Paul let him go, he moved back a step. "Wait a minute. Relax…shhh…" he hushed the boisterous man. "We don't know that for sure. We could be jumping to conclusions and way off base." Finn began to pace while he thought of every crazy scenario possible. "For all we know, Mark was taken because he was losing it. When was the last time you saw him?" When Paul only shrugged, Finn said, "I saw him a few weeks ago, and he did not look good. He was all twitchy and picking scabs. I mean, geez, he looked like a tweaker. Maybe they took him then. You've seen too many people go batty or attempt suicide, and then we get gassed, and they are gone, never to return. It could be a coincidence."

Paul had been rubbing his hands together and grinning manically through the speech. "All right, let's go search out some of the other botanists. There had to have been what, thirty or more on the ship, right?"

Finn nodded, catching on to Paul's thoughts.

"Let's enlist the other guys and start asking after them all. Are they still here? Do others around them notice that they go missing and come back later?" Paul elbowed Finn in the side. "At least we're having some fun now, right!"

Finnegan, feeling elated with the new prospects, was still sad that Helen wasn't with him, and he could only hope that she was still alive and he would see her again one day.

8. The Men, The Women

When Montana opened her eyes the morning after her talk with Finn, her first emotion was sadness. Helen was gone now. Then the conversation rose to the forefront of her memory, and her heart raced. There was a way into the museum. She sprung off her platform and ran down the hall, dodging people who said nothing. She only smiled as she darted past, straight to Alma's chamber. The first thing she noticed was that the elderly woman had followed her direction and taken the sacks to her bed as well. Only she did not have them in the tumultuous jumbled, messy pile, but a neatly folded triple padded layer underneath her body.

Not wanting to scare her, Monty slowed her pace. "Alma?" she whispered.

Alma blinked. "Hmm?" Her head turned to the bright-eyed little girl beside her, and her lips parted, showing her white teeth. "Monty, good morning." She sat up and ran her hand through her grey waves of hair. "You look awfully chipper today."

Monty bounced on the balls of her feet. Now that Alma was awake, she was ready for adventure. "Finn told me about the way into the museum." She did a jig, wiggled her hips, and flailed her arms about, finding it hard to contain her energy. "Can we go? Can we see if it's true?"

Alma had spoken with Finnegan the night before and was surprised he had told the child. She knew things were going to move faster now, because containing a child's excitement was akin to holding a firecracker from bursting. But then she thought perhaps it was for the best; they had nothing to lose. "First, we have to find a way into the woman's area and talk to Dartania. Remember that mean lady who kicked us out?"

Monty's face fell into a frown. "Oh, ya. I never thought of her. Maybe I can find Dartania, and she can help us."

Alma ruffled the girl's hair. "Yes, that is something that we need to do. And you know Brenda Kelly, right? She wants to help us too. Let's go get her, and we can sit and talk about how best to proceed, okay?"

Monty continued to dance about the room, repeating, "Best to proceed, best to proceed, best to proceed," in a singsong fashion, and flowed behind Alma as she exited the room.

They headed left to the circular tunnels that would lead them through the museum and over to the next section where Brenda stayed. Monty did not stop to admire anything on route today, as her attention was drawn to a new adventure. Emerging out the opposite side, they simultaneously spotted Dartania as she headed down a different section.

Alma prodded Montana on the shoulder. "Go see if you can get her to stop and talk to me."

"Okay," Monty squealed and raced off. "Dartania, wait!" she called out as she traced the young woman.

While Alma slowed her pace, she could only hope that Monty was able to keep her from bolting off again. As she neared the next turn, she could faintly hear the two voices but not enough to make out what they were saying. Then to her surprise, Monty came around the bend pulling Dartania, as though leading a blind person. "This is Alma, and she's super nice. You'll like her, I promise," Monty said.

Alma stopped walking. Keeping her distance, she gave a quick wave. "Hi, Dartania. How are you?"

The young woman's eyes darted over Alma from head to toe, scrutinizing her, as if assessing a possible threat. "You were in my room."

Alma placed her palm over her heart, knowing that showing genuine actions would help convey her words. "I am truly sorry about that. We were looking for you, not trying to invade your space. Can we start over?"

Dartania's eyes were wide and almost perfectly round. They were a light brown with flecks of amber that even in the steady light of the tunnels somehow reflected eerily. She was lucky to have the skin tone of East Indian descent, and her olive darkness made Montana appear ghostly beside her. "Can Montana come see my collection?" was her only reply.

"Of course she can, sweetie. Can you tell us what is in your collection?"

Dartania squinted and shook her head. "No, but she can see."

"Sure, all right. What about your friend Linda? Will she let Monty in with you?"

"Linda is not my friend," Dartania spat back. "She steals from my collection. She can't tell me what to do!"

"Oww." Monty shook her hand. "You're hurting me."

Dartania released Monty. "Let's go now." She walked away from Monty and passed Alma without further acknowledgment.

Alma crouched and quickly whispered to Monty, "Go with her. I am going to find Brenda and be right behind you. Go."

Alma hurried off in the direction they were originally headed, now running through the corridors, searching for Brenda. She didn't want Monty to be too far ahead of them and have an encounter with Linda. Slowing, she turned into Brenda's pod, and the woman was laying on her platform staring that the transparent ceiling. Her head swiveled as the noise disturbed her daydreaming.

"Hurry, I'll explain on the way." Alma waved the woman out of her space and began a light jog back the way she came.

Brenda jogged alongside, holding her arms tight across her chest as she was too robust to be fast walking, never mind jogging. "Come on, tell me," she insisted.

"Montana and I were coming to talk to you about how to get into the women's area when we ran into Dartania—"

Brenda gasped. "*Thee* Dartania?"

"Yes, *thee* Dartania. She wanted to take Monty off to see some collection, but she wouldn't say what it was. She did emphatically state that Linda is not her friend. I think that is why she's come out here after all this time. She is having troubles with this woman and seeking an outsider to bond with. And who safer than someone younger and less intelligent.

"A child." Brenda gasped again.

"That's right."

"That's all well and good, but do we have to jog?" Brenda stopped, bent at the waist and gasping for breath. "I can't."

Alma stopped and leaned against the hard rock wall, also gasping. "Yes, it's been too long, hasn't it?" She pushed herself away. "Let's at least keep walking. We don't want to lose ground."

Brenda straightened, licking her lips. "Damn. Might help if we had water."

~~~~~~

Meanwhile, Finnegan and Paul had gathered up the men—even George, for if he was going to be a part of this, then he was going to work too—and they set off to inquire about the other botanists. None of them knew the actual names or connections of the botanists. Finn had only known of Mark because he'd worked so closely with Helen. On a ship of five hundred thousand people, not everyone knew each other. They did not expect this to be an easy or fun task, but it was better than sitting around waiting for nothing to happen, as they had for the past seven years. The plan was to stop every person they saw and ask if they knew of anyone missing within the last—best guess—month, and if so, what their job was on the ship. They all knew it would start raising questions and get curious inquiries back, but they hoped soon it wouldn't make a difference. They were all dreaming of freedom.

As he walked around talking to others, Finn tried to imagine what that freedom would look like. They knew before they crashed that Kepler couldn't support life on the surface. *Would they have to murder the slugs and live one floor up but still underground? How was it different up there?* All they ever saw were the slug's undersides. *Were their tunnels an exact replica of the ones they resided in now, only with the see-through floor? Now that'd be a sight,* he thought as he pictured all the humans walking around in their sack dresses, their parts bared to the empty tunnels below.

After hours of chatting with some familiar faces and many complete strangers, Finnegan made his way back to the sauna area. A few of the other men were already back, but not all. As he sat, Bertram said, "You guys were right. Every person missing recently has been a botanist."

"Yes," Finn agreed. "I found four people, who knew people missing without reason and they all worked with the plants."

"Well, I didn't find a one," George grumbled, rubbing his feet.

Preston lay back enjoying the steam and harrumphed. "I bet you didn't even ask."

"Hey, I walked for hours, I'll have you know," George whined.

"Bitching already, eh, George?" Paul's voice echoed through the chamber as he entered the space. "We were right, Finn. I talked to eight people that knew of, or heard of, missing men and women, and all within the past couple of weeks."

"All right, what can this mean?" Russell asked.

"It means the reason we have never had the atrium as a part of our ship museum down here, is because those bastards upstairs have it," Paul stated. "And my theory is that it's not doing well underground, so they needed all our people to help it thrive again."

Bertram shook his head. "Okay, that's a theory, but so what? How does knowing this help us?"

"Well," Finn added, "for starters it gives me hope that Helen is still alive, and if we can get out here, there is a chance of life."

"Oh," Bertram said simply. "I guess I've been down here too long. I never thought of those things."

"Okay, we still have to get into the women's area and see if there is a hole into the museum, and then what?" George asked. "Do you think we can start the ship? It's in a billion pieces, and underground, and spread from here to Timbuktu!"

"Look." Paul raised his voice over the others as they began murmuring. "We don't know anything yet. First, we have to verify there is a hole and see where it leads. Can we start with that?"

"Any word from Brenda or Alma yet on their progress?" Russell asked.

Finn shook his head. "Alma was not in her pod this morning when I got up, and neither was Monty, I am hoping that they went off and are working on that problem. We should just hang here until they come, see how they made out."

George pushed himself up against the wall for support, and Finn marveled at how a personality could make a person still look dumpy. They had no food for years, and George was all skin and bones like the rest of them, yet in

Finn's eye, the man had a spare tire for a belly and chipmunk cheeks.

George crossed his arms and closed his eyes. "Ya, what diff? Here, there, we wait. At least if we wait, we all hear the story at the same time."

Paul took a spot on the opposite wall. "Sure, my football game can wait."

The guys settled in, talking about earthly things, and waited for the girls.

~~~~~

Alma and Brenda had caught up enough to glimpse Dartania's extra-long flowing hair as she entered the women's area. "Monty, wait up!" Alma shouted, hustling faster.

Monty's freckled face peeked out of the opening. "Alma, come on."

The ladies breasted Monty, and in unison, they trailed after Dartania. Following her through the wider tunnels, they went unchallenged by the women they passed.

Alma dared question the young woman. "Uh, Dartania…" She paused, waiting for a reaction, and seeing her head turn back enough to catch a corner of her big brown eye, Alma continued. "How do you know we are not going to be kicked out by Linda again?"

"It's Tuesday. Linda always goes to yoga steam on Tuesday."

Brenda's lip curled up, opening her nostril comically, and mouthed at Alma, *Tuesday?*

Alma shrugged in return; she didn't know either. "How do you know it's Tuesday?"

"If yesterday was Monday, then today is Tuesday. Don't you know the days of the week?" Dartania spoke down to them.

"What are days of the week?" Monty asked, looking at Brenda.

Brenda shushed her. "Not now. I'll explain later."

"Sorry, we kind of stopped paying attention to that sort of thing here. But you did not, huh?" Alma asked, aiming to learn as much as she could about this young woman as she was allowed.

Dartania said nothing as they reached her pod. Brenda was clearly shocked at all the piles of sacks around the room, but Alma and Monty having already been there, were not.

Heading straight for the piles that reached the ceiling, the girl began taking armfuls of the clothes and placing them into new neat stacks on the floor. When she got it down to knee-high, she crouched down, slid her arms around the pile and pulled it away from the wall.

Both Alma and Brenda gasped in shock.

Monty leaned in, unsure of what she was seeing. "What is it?"

"It can't be? Can it? Is it?" Brenda exclaimed. Her fingers pressed to her thick lips, her eyes tearing up.

"You really have a way into the ship, don't you?" Alma said.

Dartania nodded. "Linda keeps stealing my stuff."

On the floor, pressed up against the wall and hidden behind the piles of their all too familiar potato-sacks, there was a hairbrush, a hand mirror, a tube of toothpaste, a pen, a Pepsi Cola bottlecap, and other various small items.

Brenda was crying now. "Can you get food? Have you found any food?" She stepped into Dartania, bumping the girl's shoulder with her oversized bosom.

Dartania's eyes narrowed, and she quickly pushed the pile back toward the wall to hide her stuff. "You're like Linda," she said.

"Oh, no, no, I'm sorry." Brenda stepped back frantically. "I'm not. I'm sorry. I just got excited is all. Alma, help me."

But it was Monty that came to her rescue. "Hey, can I see some of your things, Dartania? I've never seen anything up close before."

Alma added, "That's right. Monty was born here. She has never even touched an object, only the clothes and the pills.

Dartania straightened, her hair falling quickly from her face and down her back. "Here." She slipped onto one knee, reached behind the pile and pulled out the mirror. "See yourself. I like to look at me all the time."

Monty's fingers shook as she reached for the filigree silver handle. It was an authentic antique mirror and had a bit of weight to it for its size. As the light reflected back from the surface, she jumped, almost dropping it, and they all gasped. Then the little girl, who had never looked at herself before, caught sight of her pale, freckled cheeks and her eyes bulged. She flipped the mirror and looked behind it, as though seeking the person on the other side, then turned it back. Her fingers searched her tiny, mocha-colored freckles; she poked at her nose and her pink lips before directing the mirror to her jade-green eyes. She blinked, peered up, and down and sideways and then broke out in laughter.

Alma tousled Monty's fluffy curls. "You're beautiful, Montana. That is what we see every time we look at you."

"I'm like the art." Monty grinned wider, checking out her teeth. "Just like all the paintings we see!"

"Okay, give it back." Dartania grabbed the mirror away from the child.

"Hey, I thought you wanted me to see." Monty pouted. Now that she'd held a treasure, she wanted more. That minute was nowhere near long enough to see all she could see.

"Yes, see. Not keep. This is mine."

"And where do you go to get all this?" Brenda asked absentmindedly, peeking behind the other piles of clothes in the room.

"Gaia," Dartania said.

Alma shook her head to silence Brenda as she felt another rash question ready to burst forth. "Do you think you can show us how to get into Gaia?"

"Only if you promise not to tell Linda."

"We promise," the three practically said in sync.

"Come back next Tuesday, earlier. She'll be back soon," Dartania stated then nodded to her door. Apparently the visit was over.

"Can I please have one thing?" Monty bounced and whined.

Dartania reached behind the pile again and came out with a pen. "Only this. Keep it a secret," she said, tucking it into the child's hand.

Monty looked at it confused but cupped it tightly. Even though she had nowhere to hide it, and it stuck out of her fist like a bright blue beacon, Dartania didn't seem to notice.

"Let's go while it's safe." Alma shooed the girls. "Thank you for trusting us, Dartania. We'll see you next week."

They hurried back through the women's area, getting hit by questioning looks along the way. Once they were safe outside, Brenda was the first to say it. "How has she kept this secret so long, and why don't those dumbasses in there know what's going on?"

"I am not sure, but I suspect that Linda caught Dartania with something and is hoarding things for herself too."

Brenda threw up her arms in frustration. "All these years, is the woman daft? Did she not consider there may be an exit!"

Alma shushed Brenda as they passed a common room that was filled with people. "All right, we don't want to start a riot. Wait until we see the men."

Monty was rolling the pen in her fingers. "You, too, Monty," Alma advised. "Keep that hidden from everyone, except our group."

"Okay," Monty said, distracted. "What does it do anyway?"

"I'll show you when it's safe," Alma assured.

Once they reached the steam chamber where the men liked to meet, Alma poked her head in and, seeing the guys, waved Brenda and Monty in with her.

"Hey, there you are." Finn greeted Alma and hugged Monty, but avoided even eye contact with Brenda. "What's this?" His eyes went from the pen to Alma and back to the pen again.

"Dartania gave it to me. Can you tell me what it does?"

Alma's face lit up, and her cheeks were hurting already. "It's true, guys. She has a way into Gaia."

They broke into uproarious joy, hugging each other and slapping backs, and Finnegan even gave a quick hug to Brenda that he then had to break free of. Alma laughed, clutching her stomach, and Monty caught the giggles even though she didn't really understand why. It was just contagious.

Finn sat near Monty and asked for the pen. When she handed it to him, he pulled the cap off and rubbed the nib on the bottom of his foot. It tickled, but it wouldn't be visible to anyone. "This is a writing tool, a pen. It has ink inside, and you can write or draw with it." To demonstrate, he wrote "Monty" on the sole of his foot. "See, that is your name. I know you never got to learn how to write, but you can draw. And only do it on the floor in your room, or—" He looked around and figured the steam hid well enough. "In here."

Monty touched the ink on Finn's foot then took the pen, and as she scuttled off to play with her new toy, he called, "Don't draw on yourself like I did."

"'Kay," she answered back, already pressing the pen to the rock floor.

Now that Montana was busy, the group gathered in a sitting circle to talk about what happened in the women's area, but first, the men informed the ladies about their discovery of the missing botanists.

They discussed that weird occurrence for a while, and then, after telling the men about the hidden items and Linda, Alma said, "Everyone has to keep track of their sleeps. There is a slight possibility that she is off on her days, but if she's not, then seven sleeps from now will be next Tuesday."

"I can't believe this is real. Seven sleeps feels like an impossibility now," Bill said, rocking on his knees.

"And that's just seven sleeps until they can get back to the women's area," Paul reminded them all. "They still need to get in there and check it out, then report back to us, before we even know what we can do next."

"Okay." Preston spoke louder for attention. "In the meantime, why don't we figure out what we can do about Linda. I mean, we're not going to wait seven days every time. We need to get her on board or out of the way."

"What do you mean out of the way?" Brenda asked.

"What do you think I mean? Not there," Preston said.

"We should just tell her what's going on, that we are trying to get out of this hellhole and she should be on board," Bertram said.

"Mmm, I'm not sure about that. I think she's gone a bit off her rocker," Alma stated. "She's known about this place for a while, and she steals items from Dartania. No person in their right mind would do that. They would have told others, and word would have spread. We would all know about this by now."

"I think Alma's right," Finn said. "Let's use these few days to think about that."

Russell spoke up. "What if her sleep pattern is different from ours?"

"Ah ha, good point." Paul wagged his finger. "How about we all take turns watching the intersection from the women's area to ours. If anyone spots her, just ask her what day it is. Then we'll know for sure."

Finnegan nodded. "That's a good idea."

They all agreed and went their separate ways.

Finn and Alma moved to where Monty was busy drawing on the floor. "Let's see what you made kiddo," Finn said, peering over her shoulder and his breath held.

Like any child on Earth from ages three to eight or nine, Montana had drawn a house, with a woman, a man, a child, and a chameleon on a leash. However, these were not the stick figures of someone who had never even held a crayon before. Her details were outstanding, not perfect, not 100 percent straight, but the house had a three-dimensional porch and a neatly shingled roof—exactly like one in the museum art room. There was a porch swing that was so lifelike, you'd swear it was moving. The people were distinctly Helen, with her chestnut shoulder-length hair and her soft, gentle features, and Finnegan, with his tawny Irish locks and too-thin-but-still-muscular arms. The little girl, of course, was Monty, with her tumbled wild curls and the cocoa-colored freckles. Even the chameleon was a tiny replica of her favorite painting in the gallery.

Alma wiped a tear from her eye and hugged the child from behind. "Oh, Montana, we're getting you out of here." She then placed a kiss on the tender skin of the girl's temple and held back more tears.

9. Seven Sleeps

The group had taken turns near the tunnel into the women's area, and no one had encountered Dartania in seven sleeps. Alma gathered Brenda, requesting that Finnegan keep Monty busy and out of the way. If anything went wrong, she did not want the child anywhere near the women's area. Montana did not even pay attention to all that was happening around her, what with her new pen. She had stuck to drawing in her room as Finn had requested. However, her room was beginning to look like the graffitied cities of Earth. Luckily her pod was tucked in a corner and she wasn't open to every passerby. Every surface was drawn on, and Finn marveled at every single one of her creations. She was happier than she'd ever known, killing hours without noticing until she'd fall into an exhaustive slumber. Alma hoped that she could find some crayons or markers or anything else for the child. Her pen would be empty soon.

Alma stood on her tiptoes and kissed Finn's cheek. "Wish us luck."

"You know I do," he answered.

Brenda stepped closer. "Do I get a good luck kiss too?" She puckered her thick lips, smacking them together.

Finn slapped her shoulder. "Be careful" was all he wished her and then blended into the group of guys. The ladies went off down the tunnel, took the short jaunt left, and into the women-only section.

George paced. "Yeah, more waiting for us guys."

"Let's go catch the sermon again," Bill suggested. "Finn, this is the best chance for you to hear what the pastor has to say. I'm telling you, you might learn something that can help us get through this."

Finnegan looked to the other men. Paul shrugged; he'd never followed religion either. Bertram, Preston, and Russell all agreed with Bill.

"He does have a good point," Russell agreed.

Finn sighed. "All right, just another time-waster. Maybe it'll keep my mind off all this business."

~~~~~~

The two ladies wound their way back through the unfamiliar tunnels, but it wasn't too hard to figure out which way they needed to go. No one really paid them any mind again, and Alma slowed as they neared Dartania's pod. There was no sign of Linda, and Alma knew better than to trespass on the young woman, she rapped lightly on the outside of the cavern wall.

"Dartania?" she called out.

The olive-skinned beauty stepped elegantly out of her space, her eyes large but her expression blank. "This way," she said and turned back the way they'd come.

The women silently followed her, afraid to speak and break the promise of being led to the museum. They went through some twists and turns and took various side shoots. Alma was getting nervous; this area had many more tunnels and runs than theirs did. The ceiling was still and always transparent, and three slugs paced them the entire way. But they were of little concern, for if the young woman had been in and out of the area multiple times, as her hidden stock proved, then that meant the slugs either didn't care or didn't understand.

Dartania stopped near a dark entrance, finally turning to address her followers. "It gets narrow here. We have to go sideways. She glanced at Brenda's voluptuous chest.

"What?" Brenda said, shielding her breasts.

Dartania didn't reply and walked into the darkness.

Alma said, "Suck it in," and went in after her.

"Shit," Brenda said and turned as she followed them.

The ladies were first shocked by the darkness; they had not seen dark in years. A few seconds in, it was a bit unsettling, and then Alma wanted to stop and relish it, but Brenda was pushing up against her backside. As light began to seep in from the way ahead, they noticed there were no slugs above them, or if they were, there was no see-through walkway. Over their heads was solid dark rock, just like the floor and walls. The way narrowed, and they were forced to turn sideways. Brenda was likely being pressed from both sides, but it wasn't scary narrow, she had enough room to shimmy along.

First, Dartania popped out of the slit and into Gaia, then Alma, and Brenda at the rear.

"Oh my God." Alma covered her mouth. She felt emotions that she hadn't in years overwhelm her senses. They were standing in a steward's sleeping quarters on Gaia—not in the museum at all, but actually in the ship.

"Is that! Yes, it is!" Brenda squealed, keeping her voice low, terrified of being pulled from her new—old—surroundings and leaped headlong onto the bed. She pulled the pillow down, wrapped her arms around it, and inhaled the stale scent of laundry. She let loose and began to cry.

Alma touched Dartania's arm lightly. "Thank you, Dartania, thank you for bringing us here." She clasped her hands under her chin, biting her lip. Then she moved forward and touched the overhead bins. She caressed the smooth laminated doors. She pressed the latch and ever so slowly lifted the lid. Inside the cupboard were neatly pressed and folded first officer uniforms. She ran her fingers across the linen and rubbed the buttons between her thumb and finger.

"We must go," Dartania said, breaking the spell.

"But why! Can't I just stay here? I'll never come out. I just want to stay here." Brenda rolled her body all over the memory foam mattress.

Alma looked around quickly. There was the door leading out, a door to the tiny bathroom, and the single seat with a small surface where the crew-person would have used a memory screen. And that was the size of the room. "Do the doors lead to other areas?"

Dartania nodded.

"Okay, we'll talk on the way out. Come on, Brenda, we can't get caught."

Dartania turned and squeezed back into the slot in the wall between the makeshift desk and the bed.

Alma tore open the center drawer on the desk and was pleased to find three pens, one black, one green, and one red, and a pencil. She grabbed them in her fist and waved to Brenda. "Now."

Brenda reluctantly left the pillow and followed the women into the wall. They retraced their steps through the darkness and out into the light. Their three watchers were hovering above waiting.

Alma asked, "What's the longest amount of time you've spend in there?"

The girl didn't even have to think about the answer. "Two days."

"Two entire days? Forty-eight hours?" Brenda stumbled, flabbergasted.

"And the slugs didn't gas the place and put you back?"

"Maybe? The gas doesn't travel through there." Dartania spoke, her inflection never changed. "If they looked for me, I never saw them. The slug was still there when I came out."

This was all valuable information, and Alma absorbed it all. "Thank you, Dartania. Thank you so much."

Dartania stopped and pointed down a tunnel that wound off to the left. "You go that way now. It's a different way. Stay left, and you'll get out." Then she turned and disappeared down another offshoot.

"Ah, damn it." Brenda reached for the girl, but she was gone.

"Come on, we're fine." Alma led them left and back toward what they had been calling home for years.

~~~~~

Pastor Mayweather was already talking when the men arrived. They stayed near the back of the room and sat in their own row so as not to disturb anyone.

"The Lord is my light and my salvation. Whom shall I fear? The Lord, the stronghold of my life—of whom shall I be afraid? When the wicked advance against me to devour me, it is my enemies and my foes who will stumble and fall. Though an army besieges me, my heart will not fear; though war break out against me, and with the Savior's hand, we shall break free. Now we know what it is to be in need, and we know what it is to have plenty. We have learned the secret of

being content in any and every situation."
Mayweather turned and looked directly at Finnegan. "I can do everything through Him, who gives me strength. For we do not have a watcher who is unable to sympathize with our weaknesses." He raised his hands to the ceiling. "We have one, who in every respect, has been tested as we are." Now, his arms spread out before the crowd. "But they that wait upon the Savior shall renew their strength." His melodious voice rose in crescendo. "They shall mount up with wings in freedom. They shall run and not be weary. They shall walk and not faint. Remember not the former things, nor consider the things of old. Behold, we are doing a new thing." His voice softened once again as he lured the crowd under his spell. "Now it springs forth, do you not perceive it? He will make a way in the wilderness. And He will make rivers in the desert. And we shall see the light of day."

Pastor Mayweather continued on in this vein, of mixing various Bible verses with his own predictions. Finnegan could see how the people could easily turn what that man was saying into some sort of weird endgame. But then, any good charlatan, card reader, mind reader, or seer played the same game.

There was no cut-and-dried answer. Nothing like "Finnegan is our leader, and he will find a stairway that will lead us to the daylight." Finn eventually tuned the man out and had his own daydreams, and soon it was over. They reformed as a group and headed back toward the sauna.

"Did you feel it, Finn? He knows our day is coming." Bill nodded enthusiastically.

Not wanting to get into a weird theological argument, Finn said, "Sure, Bill, I felt something." And as they closed in on the area, Alma and Brenda came around the corner.

"Ah, what timing!" Paul exclaimed.

"I'm surprised the entire neighborhood doesn't know our business," George scoffed as he entered the steam chamber.

"No one cares, George," Paul said, bowing for the ladies to enter first.

"So?" Finn asked, seeing the fistful of pens.

Alma took a deep breath and looked like she was holding back tears. "Finn, it was incredible! We were in one of the staterooms. There was the made bed with linens and uniforms. In the cubby…pens." She showed him the now sweaty find.

"It was heaven, guys! I did not want to leave," Brenda added.

"But it's a bit tight of a passage." Alma looked about at the men. "Paul might not fit." Then she looked at Brenda and back at Paul. "Well, it's hard to say. We may have to figure out how wide you are. Perhaps tuck away your pills a few days prior, without the watchers noticing, and you can lose a couple pounds."

"Whoa, slow down there, lady," Paul said, stopping her. "You're going way too fast. What about the slugs? What happened when you went in?"

"Dartania claims she's been in there for two days at once, and they can't gas in there, and they didn't go in after her," Alma informed.

Preston nodded along. "That's handy information. If they can't gas us in there, then we should just get in and stay in."

"Can you find it again? Was it easy?" Finn asked.

Brenda shook her head. "God, no. It was confusing as hell. The walk was probably forty-five minutes, all twisty and turny and offshoots... Our area is nothing like that."

"Shit, it's always something!" George cursed.

"I'm sure if we can get Linda on our side, Dartania will lead us back again. Besides," Finn said, "we have to get all the ladies to let us through the entrance to begin with."

"I wonder if we gather outside their area, will the slugs intervene?" Bertram suggested.

Russell shook his head. "Why would they? As long as we're not physically fighting, they shouldn't."

"It doesn't hurt to try." Paul nodded in anticipation. "If they do, then we come back to the drawing board and start a new plan."

Brenda sat up straight. "Are we doing this now?"

"Why not? You got other plans?" George spat, and Brenda stuck out her tongue at him.

"No point in waiting any longer," Finnegan agreed. "We know there is an opening. We have someone that can lead us there now. Let do this."

Alma looked down at the pens. "Oh, someone should stay with Montana."

"But what if they just let us in? Then she needs to be with us," Finn said worriedly. He would not go into the ship and leave Monty out here. If things went wrong, he needed to know that he could be near her and protect her.

"Geez, we'll wait. Go get the kid," George nearly shouted.

"Wow, concerned much?" Brenda spat back at him.

"Come on, Finn, we'll go together." Alma stood, keeping the pens safe.

Once they were out of earshot of the group, Finn asked, "This is real, right? After all these years, we may have a chance of getting out?"

Alma grabbed his wrist. "Yes, Finn, it's real, and it was…" She rolled her eyes. "As Brenda said, heaven." She cleared her throat. Speaking softly, she said, "Have you given any thought to the idea that if we mess up, and Helen is still alive, that they might hurt her?"

"Of course I have, Alma. All I do is think of crazy scenarios and what they are doing to her. Is she even really alive now, or is that a pipe dream? Have they melted her mind? If we find her, will she know who we are? Look at how many times you said she went and came back and didn't remember a thing. What do they do to her? What do they use her for? All I have are questions and no answers. Maybe now, finally, we'll get some answers."

"You're right, Finn. I'm sorry." She stopped him before the entrance to Montana's room. "No matter what happens, know that I love you and Helen."

Finn's eyebrows gave a quick pinch and back up again like a crow taking flight. "I know that, Alma." He rounded the corner. "Monty!"

Monty looked up from her newest drawing. She had recreated many of the various animals she'd seen in the gallery and some odd creations of her own imagination. "Hi, guys," she said and resumed drawing.

"Look what I got for you." Alma held open her palm. The pens lay bared as colorful Christmas gifts.

Monty squealed with delight at the colors and tore them from Alma's grip so fast she never even felt them leave. The girl flopped to her bare knees on the hard floor and immediately began to add red and green to her artworks.

"Do you want to hide those away for now and come on an adventure?" Finn asked.

"Uh, no."

"What do you mean no?"

"I'm busy here." Monty pointed at the new colors.

"Oh, I guess that was a mistake," he said, addressing Alma. He looked at Monty. "We're going into the museum without you then."

"What!" She sprang up, and her new pens scattered across the floor.

Alma nodded. "He means it. We are going to go to the women's area and talk to the ladies and see if they will let us in."

Monty's smile dropped. "Oh, that mean lady won't."

"Maybe if we tell her about the museum entrance she will. Come on. Bring your colors so we can show her, and we'll try together."

Monty picked up her pens, dragging her feet and for the first time in her life being obstinate. "All right. Let's go then."

The group convened at the steam chamber and traveled two abreast through the tunnels toward the women's area. They received plenty of funny looks and a few questions but continued on without losing stride.

As they gathered just outside the entrance where only women were supposed to proceed, Alma said, "You realize it won't be long before talk spreads, and everyone is clamoring to get here."

Voices mingled as everyone voiced their thoughts. Paul whistled for attention. "For now, let's see if we can get in there. Then we'll deal with everyone else. We may pick up a few helpers, but we can't have five hundred thousand people trying to find the hole. Just keep it as low key as we can."

Everyone agreed, and George asked, "Now what?"

"One of the ladies should go in and bring Linda Walker out to us to talk," Bertram suggested.

But they never even got the chance to discuss the next step when a short, bald woman, in her early thirties or so, stopped on the opposite side of the entrance. Seeing the large group of men gathered startled her, and before anyone could stop her, she turned and ran back the way she came.

Brenda laughed, her shift bouncing along with her body. "Well that solves that then."

"Shh, shh, I hear voices," Russell pointed out.

"Let us do the talking," Finnegan said, pushing through to the head of the group beside Alma, Paul, and Monty.

Above them, the alien followers were likely jumbling together, as they had a more significant base mass than humans, and it was a comical sight if Finn had bothered to look up, which at that moment, none of them did.

"What's going on here?" Linda Walker's voice grated in everyone's ears. She stopped three feet from the exit on her side, and six or seven other women moved in behind her. Her thick arms were planted firmly on her high hips, and she kept her feet pressed tight together, as though etiquette in a dress in the 1950s ruled.

Finn held up his hands, palms out, in a universal peace gesture. "We only want to talk to you."

"About what?" Linda asked, her spooky eyes piercing the group.

Finn first looked back over one shoulder, then the other, double-checking with the group that this was what they wanted to do. Everyone nodded, *do it*. "We have found out that there is a way into Gaia—"

Those simple words brought a raucous of noise from the ladies. All voices rose as they gasped and spoke at once.

Finn raised his voice and kept talking. "Through there"—he pointed to the tunnel— "and we want to be let in to see if we can find a way to help us all out of here."

"BE QUIET!" Linda screamed for silence. The girls all hushed immediately. Next, her head tilted back as she laughed. "You must be mad." Her head straightened, and her white-and-blue-eyed stare now pierced into Finn's own soft brown ones. The color of her eyes were similar to a husky's, and there was something about that color that always made him feel off-balance. "How can you even entertain the idea that there is a way into Gaia? And in HERE," she spat, "of all places!"

Alma stepped forward. "What do you stand to gain by hiding this from everyone? We have a chance to get out of here."

Voices murmured through the women again, and one small voice questioned Linda. "Is that true?"

Linda waved her arm at the group outside her area. "Go back to your fantasy. Leave us be."

"Then why do you steal things from Dartania Aswar?" Brenda shouted.

Linda's mouth opened and closed like a carp out of water. "I do no such thing!"

Montana bravely pushed between Finnegan and Paul. She held out her hand, her tiny fist opening, and showed them her new prized possessions, her colored pens.

"Where did you get those?" "Are those pens?" "How?" "Let me see!" The women all shouted questions as they saw the treasures in the child's possession. They pushed past Linda, knocking her to the side, and rushed at Monty.

Monty squealed at the sudden onslaught of people, and Finnegan swooped her up into his arms. Everyone was yelling something at someone, and the groups became a mixed jumble of bodies. In the background, Linda was screaming at her women, trying to regain control.

Then the gas came.

Finn had enough time to spin toward the cavern wall and hunch down over Monty as the air began to cloud.

~~~~~

Finnegan was mesmerized by the chestnut-haired beauty, as she glided across the floor from one person the next. Her face, even in the false setting of artificial life, was at complete peace. He had never seen anything like it. It was as if her very being radiated the fountain of youth. Standing from his chair near the screen, where he'd been watching an old hunting show and eating his reheated three-course meal, he moved to her, his dinner and show all but forgotten and left behind. He didn't have to think about the steps he was taking or watch where he was going; his body was tethered to this woman. In that instant, he understood love at first sight. There would be times in the subsequent nights where he would ponder that day. He did not believe in love. He was not a pushover or a romantic fool. How could an emotion change one's entire world in the blink of an eye? But he would not fight it. Hell, he didn't want to. And now, watching her, he swore her teeth actually sparkled as her mouth parted in laughter and that sound sent shivers down his spine. As she was bending to give the elderly woman a carnation, for that was what she was doing when Finn saw her, giving people flowers, he reached out and plucked it from her thin fingers.

"Allow me." He knelt before the elderly woman. "Enjoy the beauty of life, my lady." He handed the now twittering woman the blue flower. Then he stood and hooked his arm through the flower girl's and said, "Let me help you with that." And seeing her cinnamon-colored eyes dance with his brashness, Finn felt his heart swell and knew from this day forth, she was his girl.

His heart now pounded in his chest as the dream of his first encounter with Helen washed away, and his eyes opened to the light. He sat and spun his legs off the platform. "God, I hope I get to see you again."

It felt like a different type of Groundhog Day today, for before when they lived the exact same day over and over, some had joked about the silly old movie. Now, they had something to live for and something to fight for, and being set back at every turn was truer to the movie. Finn shook his head. *What funny thoughts to be having.* "Focus," he said out loud and looked up. Tattoo was there as always.

He was about to head out and check on Monty when Alma poked her head into his space. "Hey. How are you feeling?" she asked, her grey waves of hair slightly flat, indicating they had most likely slept their standard seven to eight hours.

"Not tired and very frustrated. How are you? Where's Monty?" He looked past her shoulder, expecting to see the child, but she wasn't there.

"She's fine. Not happy…but fine." And as Finn opened his mouth to ask what happened, Alma stopped him. "They took her pens away, but she's still with us."

Finn slid off his bunk. "That's a relief; I was worried for a sec." He moved instinctively to the small divot in the wall and fished out his daily pill. "Should she come with us?"

Alma shook her head. "No, she's bundled up in her pile of sacks, crying. I don't think listening to all of us talk politics and schemes will be good for her."

"All right. Let's gather everyone and go talk."

They picked up George first, who much to Finnegan's ire, did not even inquire as to the well-being of his own daughter after the gassing. When they arrived at Paul Smythe's area, they found Bill and Russell there with him.

Finn poked his head through the opening. "Hey, guys, coming out? We can't all fit in there." Russell shuffled awkwardly between Bill and the wall. He was a pilot, so Finn knew he had to be uncomfortable in his "dress." Pilots spent most of their days in their pants uniforms. Russell never really looked relaxed and was currently tugging at the bottom of his shift. "I don't think we need to keep hiding out in the sauna. Clearly, the aliens watch us, but they can't understand us. Let's meet in a larger common area."

"We have to find the others first," Alma said.

"Let's just head there for now." Paul stepped out to the corridor. "That's where everyone knows to meet, and then we can change the location from here on out. Agreed?"

Finn shrugged. It made no difference to him. He just wanted to get on with it.

Sure enough, as they arrived at the stem chamber, Bertram, Brenda, and Preston were already there talking. The others joined, and they sat in a circle in the center of the room—Finnegan, again, sure to always place someone between himself and Brenda.

Brenda covered her mouth as a burst of laughter was about to spring forth. Drawing looks from the group, she said, "I feel like a little man in a long coat should step out and say 'hear ye, hear ye.'" With her hands on her hips and her chest thrust even farther forward than it needed to be, Brenda pantomimed a stiff town crier.

"Real cute," George grumbled.

Bill joined her frivolity, miming her motions. "Good one, Brenda. I like it."

George rolled his eyes. "You would."

Bill looked at him questioningly. "What's that sup—"

Paul stopped the arguing with a loud throat-clearing. "Knock it off. We have things to discuss."

"Yes, what are we going to do about Linda Walker, for one," Finn said.

George thumped his fist into his thigh. "Let's draw her out and bash her head in. That way, when we wake up after they gas us, she'll be gone for good."

"There will be no bashing anyone's head in," Bertram voiced immediately.

"Perhaps yours," Brenda mumbled low enough that no one really heard.

"We need serious thought here, people," Finn said.

"I've been thinking about this." Alma spoke with a soft tone as usual, but everyone listened intently. "For whatever her own reasoning is, she doesn't want this life to change. We can speculate until we're blue in the face why, but that is not important. And it won't help us. Therapy takes years. We do not have that luxury." The group made various agreement noises at the statement, and Alma pressed on. "There is a narrow space that leads from the cave and into the ship. There is no transparent ceiling from that point on. If we can lure her into the tunnel, or even all the way into Gaia, we can tie her up. They can't see in the ship, and they can't gas us once we make it in, therefore if we leave her on the state bed, she'll be safe and comfortable."

Bill lifted his hand like a child in school and began to talk. "Before I came here, I took the liberty of speaking with the Pastor…"

A few of the group members groaned at this, Finn being one of them.

"No, listen," Bill said, pressing on. "It makes sense now. When I told him about Linda and asked why she wouldn't want to help us, he quoted me a passage. '*Luke twelve fifteen. Then He said to them, beware, and be on your guard against every form of greed; for not even when one has an abundance does his life consist of his possessions.*' Don't you see?" He implored the group. When no one responded, he said, "Linda is holding this for herself in greed."

"Okay, Bill, but how does this help our situation?" Finn asked.

"I-uh-well..." Bill stammered.

Russell interjected on Bill's behalf. "I think what our little friend is trying to convey is that we should turn to the pastor, as he has a good grasp of the situation."

Paul stood, towering over them. "I say we go with Alma's plan. Lure the bitch into Gaia, truss her up, and get on with the show."

"Sure, and who is going to lead her to the tunnel? And who is going to be in there to tie her up? And then what?" George said, his fingers picking away at his toes while he spoke.

"We are going to have to get Dartania to bring her to the tunnel, and Brenda and I will be inside, ready to grab her. That means we have to wait until Tuesday again when she won't be around, so we can slip in," Alma said, laying out her plan.

Bill was skeptical this time. "What if Dartania doesn't want to help?"

"You're her uncle." Finn waved at the man. "Talk to her. Explain that we need her in on this. The fact that she hates Linda should be a deciding factor."

A small voice carried from the entranceway. "I can help too."

"Monty." Finn peered past Bill's shoulder to the small silhouette across the room. "How long you been there, sweetie?"

Montana walked in and went to straight to Alma's side. "I want to see Helen. I miss her."

Alma took the child's hand in her own and pressed the baby soft flesh to her lips. "You can help."

"She can?" Paul said stunned. "What is this squirt going to do?"

"Monty is a fast runner. She can zip through those tunnels like the roadrunner and be the bait," Alma stated, and Montana slipped her arms around the woman's neck, sinking into the natural cup between her folded legs. Alma snuggled the warm creature to her breast and sighed. She was going to miss this.

"I think we have a base plan." Paul paced and made sure everyone was up on their end of things. "Bill, make sure you get to Dartania soon. On Tuesday, she and the kid will need to get Linda to follow them to the tunnel. Then, inside Gaia, Alma and Brenda are going to tie her up. Once that's accomplished, come get us, and we all go."

"Holy crap. I can't believe we're getting out of this hell hole!" Brenda shimmied on her bum, rejoicing.

"Calm down." Finn stood and moved away from her even farther. "We don't know yet how far into Gaia we can even get, or what's in there when we do."

"Still better than living like walking zombies until we die," Russell called back as he exited the room.

Paul let out a hearty country whoop and did a jig, his bare feet giving off a dry sandpapery sound, even in the dampness of the steam.

"Now just to stay sane for six more days," Finn said and turned to Monty. "Want to go see the art gallery again?"

Monty shook her head and climbed out of Alma's lap. "Can I tell you about my art?"

Finnegan's heart danced in his chest. He wished Helen had been here to see how talented the girl was. Then he berated himself, *Helen would see, when they escaped and Montana had the freedom to draw what she wanted, wherever she wanted.* "I would love that. Let's go." He hooked Alma's arm in his, and the three walked off, leaving the rest of the group to do as they pleased.

10. Hoopla

Dartania opened her eyes to darkness. She lifted her hand to her eyes, blocking the light. She hated it when they were put to sleep involuntarily, for she was never able to curl up into her preferred fetal position, buried under the shifts. Blinking away the light, she moved from her platform and reset her makeshift blankets into a jumbled pile. Her eyes scanned the piles of sacks along the walls; they were all just as she had left them last. As she was taking her regimented meal, voices carried from the tunnels gaining volume.

A voice pierced her silent chamber. "What did you do?" Linda yelled, her bare feet sounding like flippers at the poolside cement as she turned into Dartania's space. "Why did you tell those strangers about our secret?" Her cheeks flared as she clenched her jaw in frustration.

"I have told you before to stay out of my room. This is my room." Dartania stood tall and motionless.

"Do you know what you've don—" Linda held her words, listened for a second, then gasped and resumed in a hurried, hushed tone. "You got them excited."

Dartania stepped closer to the wall and touched the tallest pile of sacks. All her possessions were hidden by this pile, and no one was supposed to be in her room. Now, the women pushed through the entrance, filling it, stumbling and shoving each other. They knocked into her, into her piles, into her bed. Not knowing how to handle all the people at once, she pressed into the stack, pushing her arm through the middle and rubbing her fingers over the course material.

The voices were overwhelming, all trying to talk at once, until one woman let out a shrill whistle. "Quiet!" she called out. The sound lowered to a tolerable hush. "Linda." The woman named June got down to business. "Is what those people said true?"

A chorus of raised voices erupted again.

"It was all her fault." Linda's long bony finger flashed over the shorter women's heads at Dartania.

"Bitch," a short woman said.

"How can you blame a child?" said another.

"Yeah?" a chorus agreed.

"It's true?" June asked again, looking from Linda to Dartania, and she pushed through a few bodies to get closer to the young woman. "Is it true, Dar?" She knew not to touch the girl and stared directly into her honey-brown eyes, commanding attention.

"I found a safe place to hide, yes," Dartania admitted but gave no further information.

Murmurs rose in volume once again. "Take us there." "Is there a way out?" "Where is it?" Hot bodies bumped and jostled against each other in the confined space.

Dartania's skin began to flush, her breathing grew rapid, and her eyes widened to bovine proportions. She needed to get away. As the crowd started to throw questions and accusations back at Linda, who was pushed into a corner and rapidly digging herself into a deeper hole, Dartania slowly sidestepped past woman after woman until she was out in the crowded corridor. As soon as she was free of the last body, for every woman in the area had to have been crammed in the tunnel aiming to learn the truth, Dartania ran. There were too many people in her space and she needed out.

Her hair lifted behind her, a silken mane or a raven's wings, beating the still air with its strands. While above her, the watcher flew along keeping a comfortable pace. She passed empty pods, empty common rooms, and empty steam chambers. Without thought to which turn needed taking, or which tunnel was left or right, she ran and ran and ran.

~~~~~

A few nights and days had passed, or so they assumed. Sleeping was becoming harder now that they had plans to look forward to. Finnegan knew he was only resting a few hours at the most, and he'd be up pacing or off searching for another sleepless soul. They hadn't been this restless since they'd first awakened underground. Monty was on the opposite spectrum of the scale. She had only known one way of life. Her underground family had taught her, telling her stories, taking her to the museum. Life truly revolved around her. Now, she seemed depressed. She was the one hiding in her room, didn't want to go to the museum, didn't want to hear more stories, wanted Helen back, her pens back, and wanted her life to go back to the way it was before.

Needing a change, Finnegan went off in search of the guys. He found Bill, Bertram, and Paul in the last place he wanted to be, the pastor's chamber. Finnegan stopped in the doorway, with his mouth open in surprise, and the Pastor looked up.

"Join us please." He motioned toward the center of the room.

Finn begrudgingly entered the room and nodded a greeting to the guys. "Didn't mean to interrupt. I am just getting antsy."

"Aren't we all."

Pastor Mayweather kept his eyes on Finn. "I know you are a non-believer, and you do not have to believe in God to know there are always forces working in unison. Am I correct?"

Finn was taken aback. He hadn't expected the man to come right out and start lecturing him. "What does it matter, Carl?" He was not going to afford the man his title.

Mayweather closed his eyes, cupped his hands at his waist, and recited. "He who keeps a royal command experiences no trouble, for a wise heart knows the proper time and procedure. Ecclesiastes eight five." His eyes opened, eerily directed at Finn's own. "The time is soon, and you are the one to lead us from here. These people around you know that, you know that. Whether conscious of it or not, you have always known in your heart that you will have a new beginning. We will all have a new beginning, through you." He reached out, placing two fingers directly over Finn's rhythmic heartbeat.

Finn was about say, "Do you believe this guy," when he noticed the three other men nodding and agreeing.

Paul was the first to add something to the conversation. "It's true, man. Bill here"—he clapped a large mitt on the smaller man's shoulder, causing Bill to flinch and grimace simultaneously—"may have a connection to Dartania, and I may have the muscle, but you have the charisma that all eyes turn to in the time of need. We need you to guide us out and up."

Finn pushed the pastor's hand off his chest, and said, "Let's say I believe you for a second. We already know there's a hole into Gaia, but that's all we know. What are your *'insights'* after that? Can you share those details? Because they may be the most important ones."

Head held high, the pastor countered, "Ecclesiastes nine twelve. Surely, no one knows his appointed time. Like fish that are caught in a deadly net, and like birds that are caught in a snare, just like them, all people are ensnared at an unfortunate time that falls upon them suddenly. However, Leviticus twenty-six six. I'll give peace in the land so that you'll lie down without fear. I'll remove wild beasts from the land, and not even war will come to your land. Trust in what's to come, Finnegan. Go do what needs to be done."

"I'm done," Finn said then turned and walked out.

Paul and Bertram followed, but Bill stayed behind to talk with the pastor more.

"Hey, wait up," Paul called out.

Finn looked back but kept on walking. "Why do you listen to him and his Bible mumbo jumbo?"

Paul took two giant strides, catching up to the slender man, and was about to tell him something when a large group of women came around the corner toward them.

Both groups stopped.

The head of the ladies spoke first. "Can we talk?"

Finn cocked his head. He recognized a few of the faces from the other day in the woman's area before the confrontation transpired. "Of course we can. We're all in this together. Let's find an empty pod to talk in," he said as other people entered the tunnel and needed to skirt past. They already had enough members of the escape club, he didn't need any more.

The group moved together until they spotted an empty chamber, and they slipped in. June introduced everyone around and then said, "We confronted Linda Walker yesterday, we believe you. That there may be a way out. And we all want out. The problem is, Dartania disappeared during the melee, and we can't find her."

"SHIT!" Paul roared, and everyone flinched at the sudden outburst. He gripped at his hair and began pacing. "She is the only one that knows how to get there."

"Calm down," Finn said, addressing the big man. "I am sure she'll resurface soon. The question is…what about Linda?"

A short woman with a crooked smile named Swoozy piped up. "None need to worry about that bitch none more."

Finn raised a brow, but it was Bertram that spoke up. "What did you do to her?"

"Well they can't have hurt her, Doc, we didn't get gassed again," Finn said.

June's medium-length cropped hair flopped in her eyes as she nodded vigorously. "We're not the hurting kind. You're right. It was just a thousand against one. What choice does she have?" She shrugged.

"Good, good," Bertram mumbled.

"Now what? We just wait for Dartania to resurface and then get her to lead us out? Simple as that?" Paul questioned.

"I suppose so," Finn said. "We'll have to tell the others. And you ladies will keep us posted if she returns to her room?"

"Yes. I am just curious"—June's eye's locked with Finn's, demanding honesty—"because we never got the information from Dartania. Do we know how far it goes? How much of Gaia do we have access to? Is there an escape plan? We would like to know what you know."

The women around her agreed.

"We really don't know any more than you do. We had only received news of the entrance a few weeks or so ago, and because it is in your section, we couldn't go in and check it out," Finn said.

June tilted her head. "Why didn't someone just come in and tell us to look then?"

Paul spoke up. "We needed to be sure it was true before we raised false hope. There are enough crazies down here, without that added in."

Finn nodded. "And then when Alma attempted to go find out, Linda stopped her twice."

"See!" Swoozy's arms flew up in exasperation. "I tols ya she was a lying bitch. When that old lady gots kicked out, Linda tells us the lady was a doomslayer. No true. No true." She smacked June's shoulder.

"Doomsayer she means," June clarified for the group, "and yes, Linda has always been a bit of a control junkie in our section. But with so little to hold our interest, and no trouble to get into, we mostly let her be. This." She stabbed a rigid finger into the palm of her other hand. "This is different. This is our possible new future we're looking after."

"We still need Dartania to show us where this entrance is, because if after all these years not one other person has spotted it, it can't be that easy to find. We have wait for her. Then all we can do is go into Gaia and take it from there," Finn said, choosing to ignore the comments about Linda. It was none of his business.

June took two quick steps toward Finnegan and threw her thin arms around his neck. She stretched up on her toes to raise her head above his shoulder and pulled him tight to her chest. "Thank you, Finn. Thank you." When she released him and turned, he saw tears running down her cheeks. "Come on, girls, let's go set up watch." June waved her troop out of the chamber.

As soon as they were out of earshot, Paul said, "Do you think we can trust them?"

That thought had never occurred to Finn, but why would it? What did the women have to gain by going into Gaia alone? "What do you think they're going to do, Paul? Fly away on us? You really need to stop thinking the worst of people."

"Hey, that's not fair. You haven't been screwed over by women the way I have," Paul countered. An entirely different conversation ensued, and as they were headed back to tell the others what they had just learned, once again, gas began to fill the corridor.

Bertram sat against the wall and sighed. "Not again" was all he was able to say.

~~~~~~

"Wake up," the voice cooed in his ear, close but soft, a whisper of breath, the words almost discernible.

Finn held his eyelids shut, and the whisper came again. This time, it carried the scent of vanilla, and he smiled. He let his eyes open just enough to see the edges of his own eyelashes and the champagne-pink hue of Helen's lips. As they moved, her coral tongue would tease between the tips of her teeth, and he was lost. He reached out and pulled her to his mouth. Their tongues danced a sweet tango that invigorated not only his body but his heart as well. Helen laughed into his throat as they rolled and blended into one.

"I love you, heart and soul," Finn whispered to her, and she whispered it back.

The vision faded, and Finn's heart sank once more, as reality washed away his dream. He stared up at the tattooed tail above his head. "If I don't find her, I'm done. You know that, right?"

Not receiving a response of any kind, and not expecting to, Finn rolled off his platform and set off to restart the day.

11. Are we there yet?

It felt like too long since Finnegan had spent any time with Montana, and after the last two gassings, he needed to see how she was holding up. As he was headed toward her pod, Alma and Monty came around the bend.

"Finn!" Monty ran at him and jumped into his arms.

He gave her a big kiss on the cheek. "Kiddo, you're cheerful today. It's nice to see you."

"We're going back to the art display now. Do you want to come?" Alma said with a squint, a quick glance at the child, and a shake of her head.

Finn deciphered her clues as she needed alone time to head-shrink the child and replied, "I promised I'd catch up to the guys for a meeting. Can I see you two after?"

Monty wriggled to be put down. "Okay. Later, Finn." She looked at Alma. "Hurry up." Then she proceeded to race off.

Alma sighed. "Poor child. She's never had to deal with this many emotions before, but she's strong. Eventually she'll level out."

"Is she going to be all right?" Finn asked, concerned.

"Of course she will. You go, and we'll talk later. I got tidbits of the story about Linda from Bertram, but I know we all have lots to discuss."

"That we do. Later." Finn gave the woman a quick peck on the cheek and turned to go gather the men.

He found Paul, Bertram, and George in the steam room talking.

"Anyone know why we were put out this time?"

Everyone responded negatively, and they were pondering the situation when Bill came flying into the room. "Dartania's back, and that crazy woman tried to kill herself," Bill said while panting.

"Who, Dartania?" Paul asked.

"No, Linda!" Bill spat and headed back down the tunnel.

The guys looked quizzically at one another and then proceeded after Bill. It no longer was an issue for them to walk into the women-only area. Word was spreading through the colony that an escape plan was in the works, and although no one knew the details, excitement was building and rules went to the wayside. Bill raced down the tunnels, past the women—who did not question them—past large chambers filled with watching eyes, past the nude steam rooms, and finally to his niece's old safety zone. Her room.

Dartania stood outside the doorway to her pod, arms crossed tight over her chest, and her head bowed so her face was hidden in the folds of her raven tresses. The men said nothing to her as they followed Bill into the room.

It was a disaster. All her meticulously piled sacks were strewn across the floor or hanging off the platform. It was as if a tornado of beige fabric had lifted from the floor, spun in a whirlwind, and then dropped dead wherever they may have been. The shocker was the blood. A sizable, sticky, congealing pool lay dead center. There was an outward spatter of a tumultuous murder scene. Blood traced the clothes, the walls, and the transparent ceiling. Red imprints of feet, toes, and a partial heel here and there, like a crazed dance number, marked the stone floor.

"What happened here?" Finn gasped and was careful not to step in any of the blood and add to the footprints.

Behind them, June spoke. "When we came out to find you, apparently Linda became enraged. I can only recount what I was told…"

Swoozy stepped past June. "I saw'd it. Horrible, I tells ya. I weren't far off when I hear'd shouting, and I came to see

Linda in da rage. She was trowing clothes into da center of da room, screaming Dartania da traitor. One of da ohder ladies tries ta calm her down, and Linda push her away like a rag. All da stuff Dartania saves dhad be hidden against the walls, behind da clothes. Linda dwas grabbing stuffs, holding tit up the sky and yelling at da slugs. It dwas terrifying to see. She compledly lost her min'. Thatds when she found da fork." Swoozy shuttered, hugged her arms, and continued. "She'd stabbing herself wit dit and says, 'Why ya didnd takes me?'"

Bertram knelt to the blood pool, looking but not touching. "She did this to herself with a fork?"

Swoozy and June nodded. Other women gathered around the doorway listening. "Luckily, Dartania wasn't here. She only just got back after they gassed us."

"I am surprised they let her get as far as she did before they gassed her," Finn said.

"I bet they had no idea how easy it would be with a weapon," Paul added, and when people turned to him, he said, "Well, we've never had possessions before, right?"

The crowd parted, and Pastor Mayweather appeared in the doorway. He made the sign of the cross and said, "The Lord is close to the brokenhearted, and He delivers those whose spirit has been crushed."

Finn stepped toward the small man, his fists clenched. "Did you predict this, too, pastor?" he spat.

Mayweather's wide-set eyes didn't even blink. He responded, "The heart is deceitful above all things, and desperately sick. Who can understand it?"

"You're unbelievable. You know that?!" Finn pushed past him and out into the hallway and turned to Dartania. He spoke softly. "Will you take me to the tunnel?"

"She took all my stuff." Dartania's head slowly raised, her hair parting like a beaded curtain. Her eyes had shifted from a warm brown color to the raven black of her hair, but as she blinked at Finn, they flicked back to a shade of pale coffee. "She was in my room."

"Yes, she was," he agreed with her, "but if you show me where the entrance to Gaia is, we can go get it all back for you."

Dartania kept her arms tight to her own body, and began moving forward. The women moved aside as she passed, with Finn directly behind her. They turned and followed too.

Soon, everyone was following a line that probably stretched for miles, and the people at the end of the line didn't even know who they were following or why; they were just compelled. The trek was filled with whispers and murmurs, but no one raised a voice or attempted to move off.

When they finally reached the narrow slit in the cavern wall, Dartania dropped her arms and shuffled into the space.

Finn turned to the tunnel filled with bodies behind him and addressed the women. "Please let me go in and check it out before everyone starts trying to cram in here and we end up trapped in a position we can't escape from."

A voice yelled out, "Aren't we already?"

It received a chorus of agreement. However, they all truly understood the situation, and no one pressed to continue. A few feet back, and towering over most of the ladies, was Paul shaking his head; Finn didn't think there was any way he was fitting in that thin crevasse.

Finn looked to June. "Keep them calm. I'll be right back." He turned and entered the darkness. After only a few steps, he leaned his head against the rock. It felt good to be without light. He'd never truly known how much he missed it. He desired to sleep then, but there were more exciting finds ahead. He forced himself to keep moving on. Not long after, a dim light reached his eyes, and he was exiting the tunnel through a tear in the side of the ship.

As he left the rock and entered the steward's cabin, his heart flipped in his chest. He couldn't believe it was real. His bare feet touched the specialized rubber floor. It was cooler than the rock, and an instant chill raced up his spine. Goosebumps popped up on his arms, and all the hair stood on end. There was no stopping it; laughter bubbled out of his throat, and he raised his hands. It was akin to standing in the cool rain after the hottest day of the year had just melted the world. Sensations that had been dormant for years coursed through his body. He inhaled the stale smell of an old life. He turned and touched the bed, the wall, and the cabinets, grabbing the handles and pulling them open. Next, he looked up, ready to see Tattoo above, watching him, judging him, perhaps mocking him that he was dreaming again. And when saw only the ceiling of the ship, and spotty lighting, he silently rejoiced. There were no watchers here, and he felt free at last. Wanting to see more, he walked toward the tiny cubicle where the bathroom would be, and only then did he realize Dartania wasn't in the room.

Finn went to the door that should lead out into the crew section's hallway and paused for a moment. He almost wanted to say a prayer, but as a non-believer, that made no sense. Plus, if the girl wasn't in the room, then that meant there were other rooms beyond this one. He opened his eyes and activated the thumb sensor. The door slid into the wall. There was still some power. Sure enough, before him was the hallway, and across from that, another room, and to the left, more rooms, to the right, rooms. He wanted to let out a loud whoop and go running up and down the corridor in childish delight, but he knew he could not. He had to restrain himself, for now was not the time to draw attention where it need not be.

He did call out, in an even, not overly loud voice, "Dartania?" He looked left and right. There was no response, and the ship was silent. Knowing that she had been here many times before, he wasn't concerned, and he turned to go back to the people.

Going back was the hardest thing he'd had to do in his life. Now that he had a taste of where they all belonged, he did not want to return to the constant light, no food, no clothes, and rock. He had to get the others. They needed to work together. He couldn't just abandon them.

As Finn moved back through the crevasse and returned to the light, everyone cheered and then the questions flew. He held up his hands for silence. He scanned the faces around him. Everyone had the same expression, the yearning and sadness for it to be true, so he spoke. "It is real, guys. This takes us to Gaia."

The room broke in a cacophony of cheers, high fives, whistles, and crying. He waited a few minutes for the voices to die down, glancing up at the jumble of slugs above, noting they hadn't moved at all and continued. "We don't know yet if there is a way out completely. Or how much of the ship is intact here. What we need to do is take a few people and launch an expedition to investigate first."

That statement received some boos.

"Okay, let's go," one woman called out from the crowd, causing a wave of agreement.

Paul had already moved to the opening where Finn stood, to act as a bodyguard if needed. "Wait a minute here, ladies." His tenor broke the spell. "If you all want to escape our prison for good, there has to be a proper plan of action. We can't all flit about and do whatever we want."

June nodded her understanding and joined in. "The men are correct. Let us come up with a system to remember exactly where this spot is. When the time is right, every person underground will be able to find the way out."

Finn nodded. "Thanks for that. I'll gather my group, and we will let you know as soon as we do."

June winked. "Let's do this." She walked through the ladies, talking and touching arms and pulling them with her, away from the opening.

Bertram smiled. "That woman has a way about her."

"Way to go, Bertie!" Paul smacked the doctor too hard on the shoulder, knocking him off balance.

"We have bigger fish to fry," Bertram grumbled. "Are we going to know how to get back here?"

"Yes, there are specific markers along the way," Finn said. "Besides, I trust that June will have a system in place. Let's get this show on the road."

Paul sat down against the wall near the opening. "You guys go and gather the others. I am going to stay here to watch the entrance, and then we'll be sure you know how to get back again."

"If that's what you want," Finn said.

Paul closed his eyes. "Stay here, walk there, it's no diff." He jabbed his thumb over his shoulder. "Going in there is the deal. Go, hurry up. I'm anxious to get in there."

Bertram went off to find Bill, George, and Russell.

Finnegan turned down his usual route and entered the museum in search of Alma and Montana. Approaching the ladies, he called out, "We have news."

They turned at the sound of his voice, and both greeted him with hugs. He didn't want to talk of Linda's suicide in front of the child. He only told them that they knew how to get into the ship and everyone was gathering to explore.

Monty tucked her tiny hand into his and looked up at him with wide, jade-green eyes. "Will we be leaving here?"

Finn placed a cool kiss on her forehead. "First, we are going to go explore inside Gaia." He pointed to the rooms as they walked back out of the museum. "You'll get to actually touch all this. You'd like that, wouldn't you?"

She bounced on her toes. "Oh, yes! I want to touch the things." Her trepidation fell away, replaced with elation. She was ready to explore and learn new things.

"Do we have any plans being laid out for escape?" Alma asked.

Finn shook his head. "At this juncture, I thought it best to do an expedition into Gaia first. We need to learn how much is accessible and which sectors. That is why we are gathering the original group. Once we check it out, we'll come out and talk to everyone, or as many people fit in the surrounding area, and take it from there."

Alma was smiling broader than Finn had ever seen. "This is surreal. I can only imagine not being trapped any longer."

Finn shook his head. "We won't have too much longer. I promise."

As they made their way back to what used to be the women's area, others were migrating there too. The word was spreading, and everyone was heading out to see if it was true. They discovered, as they took the long walk back, that June had left one woman as a directional post at every offshoot and every deep corner. There was no chance they were going to lose the entrance again.

12. The Expedition

Moving through the now crowded tunnels, Finnegan and the girls returned to the chamber where the fissure was. They found Pastor Mayweather conducting a sermon for his captured gathering. The room was silent as all ears were enthralled by his prophecy.

"Not only that, but we also boast in our sufferings, knowing that suffering produces endurance, endurance produces character, and character produces hope. Now, this hope does not disappoint us because God's love has been poured into our hearts by the Holy Spirit, who has been given to us. And we know that all things work together for good to them that love God, to them who are the called, according to His purpose." His hands locked in prayer form and raised to the clear ceiling above. "Commit to the Lord whatever you do, and He will establish your plan." He spotted Finnegan and raised his arms. "And our new savior arrives."

The room erupted into cheers. Finn felt his face burn with embarrassment and called out, "Enough!" When the room quieted to a murmurer again, he continued. "There are six of us going into Gaia to check out what possibilities lay ahead. We need you all to be patient and let us do what is necessary so that perhaps we can, at the very least, get above ground to start."

Everyone clapped, slapped the walls, and stomped their feet. Finnegan was worried that the aliens would get suspicious and pushed his way toward the opening. Bertram, Bill, Russell, June, and George were all there, ready to go. Finn gripped Paul's shoulder. "We'll find a way in for you, too, pal."

Paul slapped Finn hard on the back. "You'd better, man, I am not staying here while you all take off!" He winked. "After all, you are the promised one."

"Piss off." Finn grumbled and then said to the group, "Let's go."

The men entered the crevasse one by one, followed by June.

"Are you ready?" he asked Monty, and though her response was yes, her rapid breathing revealed her fear.

Alma took the child's other hand. "You'll be between us. There is nothing to fear. This is going to be fun." Alma gave the girl a fast kiss on the forehead and then slid into the hole, her arm stretching, pulling Monty. Finn shuffled behind her from his end. They both felt the girl's grip tighten as they entered the darkness.

"I can't see," Monty called out. Her breath grew rapid and audible. She pulled back against Alma's hand, and her head bumped into Finn's arm.

"It's okay, Monty, this is what darkness is. We can't see either, but you don't need to. Keep moving." Finn prodded her along with this hip as Alma pulled from the front. "You can see again very soon. Turn your head toward Alma, and you'll be able to see the light ahead."

"I can. I do. I see it. I see light." Relieved, she now shuffled faster, bumping into Alma's feet.

A minute later, they all exited the opening and were standing in the steward's cabin. The others had waited there for them. George was sprawled out on the bed, his face buried in the down-filled pillow. Russell had the door open, peering out into the corridor, and Bertram was in the bathroom.

As Monty's feet touch down on the rubber floor, her eyes widened. "OH," she said and then bent to rub it. It was pliable and cooler than the rock she was used to. She moved to the bed and felt the blanket hanging over the edge. "OH." She gasped again. "George," she said, prodding her dad. "Can I see?"

"Huh?" George opened his eyes, slurping spittle from the corners of this mouth; he had already gone into a doze. Seeing the kid and the others standing around looking at him, he stood and pressed the pillow into Montana's arms. "Yeah sure, kid. Here."

As Monty wrapped her arms around the pillow and buried her face in it, Alma sat on the edge of the bed. "I'll stay with Monty. She is going to go into sensory overload here. You all do what you need to do, and I can be filled in with the masses."

"Are you sure?" Finn asked, knowing that she would be as curious as they were to explore.

She smiled. "Yes, we will be just fine here." She laughed as Monty began hopping on her knees on the soft surface.

"All right, guys, you heard the lady. Let's move out," Finn said, and Bertram came out of the washroom to get instructions. "I think we should fan out, go as far and look into as many rooms as you possibly can. We have no way to tell time, when you've exhausted yourself or hit a dead end, we'll meet back here at that point to share notes. Sound good?"

Everyone nodded. They were anxious and ready.

"Don't forget Dartania is in there somewhere. Be careful not to scare her."

The men, with June, slipped single file into the old familiar corridors of Gaia. The emergency lights lit the way in spotty—some working, some not—fashion, but it was plenty to see by. Russell, George, and June went left. Bertram, Bill, and Finnegan turned right. Currently, they were in the crew housing area. Russell, an ex-captain, had been in this section before. It housed private rooms, cafeterias, entertainment centers, community washrooms, and recreational areas. It would be an exact replica of the patron's section. They knew they had a lot of ground to cover.

Separating off as soon as the corridor split, the men and woman all went on their way.

Finnegan opened room after room, and they all appeared intact. He arrived at a large oval door, and the sign above depicted a gaming room. Pressing his thumb to the pad, as he had with all the rooms, this door did not open. He pressed again harder. Nothing. He swirled his thumb around and nothing. He touched the surface of the door and felt a warp in the material. It wasn't visible to the naked eye, but the door was damaged. "First game room, off section BCG," he noted to himself and moved on.

The next sizable common area was a cafeteria. Finn peered into the dim section. There were at least a hundred round tables, with attached-stool-style seating, and each table sat six. They were suspended from the ceiling on large azure poles and did not rest on the floor. He was tempted to enter and pull open cupboards to see if there was food, but he pushed that desire down. It was not what they needed right at this moment. Continuing along the hallway, it began to bend and slope upward, or he could decide to skirt the thin wall and head down into the bowels of the ship. For now, he pressed on going up. The aliens were up, and there may be a way out. Up. That was where he wanted to be, up.

The engineers designed the ship to have transport chutes, but they required more power than Gaia currently had. They designed the curved walkways that wended in a lazy fashion closer to the exterior of the ship so one could move from floor to floor by walking. Finn wished the chutes worked to save time but was happy to have his feet on something man-made. As he climbed, he marveled at how much of Gaia was intact. After his next ten steps, he regretted that thought as he turned with the flow of the ramp and came to a dead end. The walkway ended, and he was back to staring at the tan rock wall of his seven-year prison.

"Shit." He slapped the stone and looked at the edges of the ship. Here, the edges were clean, as though sliced with a giant sharp knife through a tin can. He couldn't help but laugh as an image of the ancient commercial flashed into his mind of a Ginsu knife slicing a cola can.

Finn turned and walked back to the level below. He was trying to picture the layout of the ship, and how the upper portion could end at that precise spot but this floor could continue on, when he spotted Bill enter a room ahead. "Hey," he called out and went after the man.

When he got there, the door was closed. It was a movie theater that doubled as a window to space when a movie wasn't playing. Finn thumbed the pad, and the door whooshed aside. "Bill?"

Bill had taken one of the plush seats at the front and was staring at the blank wall. "I just need to sit in a chair again." He stared ahead not moving, and yet his wisps of hair still danced as his mouth moved. "You know, Finn? To do a normal activity. To feel the cushion against my legs and back. Now I want to sleep."

Finn walked down the aisle and sat beside the man. He was right. To sit on a soft chair, to feel the back nestling into his was remarkable. "It is wonderful, Bill, I agree." He pushed himself up before he did fall asleep. "But this is only the beginning. We will have our lives back again, and the sooner we find a way out, the faster that can happen."

"All right," Bill said, "but I am sleeping here from this moment on!"

Finn laughed, slapping the man on the back. "As you wish, sir."

They resumed wandering through the empty ship. Bill continued on straight as Finn came to another walkway that meandered upward, and he hoped for better luck this time. As he walked, he knew he'd surpassed the level where it abruptly ended last time, and he was right. After a few more minutes of pressing on, the walkway opened to an enormous central hub. This was the passenger level, an area that he had traversed many times during his stay on Gaia. Checking the symbols and directional signs overhead, Finn got his bearing and turned left.

Again, he marveled at how much of their ship was still intact and his pace quickened as he turned from one hallway to the next. Finally, he made it to the section where he had been housed, and he ran straight for his assigned room. He wasn't sure why, after all they had endured and the important thing now was to find a way out, that he was drawn to head back to his own quarters. He pressed the thumb pad, and once the door slid open, he saw his belongings, and he knew.

The smell of cedar and pepper reached his nose, and a tear fell from his eye. He stepped over the threshold and back into his life. His denim pants with the worn leather belt were still slung over the back of the chair where he'd left them. He picked them up and brought the fabric to his cheek and inhaled. Quickly, with renewed vigor, Finnegan tore off the potato sack dress and jumped feet first into his slacks. He bent and twisted and wanted to do jump kicks, but there wasn't enough room in the cabin. After tossing his head back, he howled into the ceiling. Laughing to beat the band, he tore open his drawers and pulled out a white cotton T-shirt. Next, he put on socks and dug out an old pair of sneakers that he kept for playing sports. He bounced, tiptoed, and mock tap-danced. He never would have thought having clothes would mean as much to him.

Now that he was fully clothed, he went back into the hallway and ran. He did not bother opening every single cabin; that would take too long. He knew the best places to scope would be the big spots. He checked the dance hall, dining hall, rec rooms, squash courts, and nightclubs. What he needed to do was talk to someone that understood the complete layout of the ship. *Russell should know*, he thought, and then he spotted another corridor that traveled upward and went for it. This one was also complete, and as he entered the next floor, he knew he was in the high roller section. The floors here were not rubberized like below but made of shiny parquet tiles. Each tile, inlaid with an intricate pattern, interwove with one another into what he was sure was a beautiful picture.

Finnegan searched for hours, until he was so tired on his feet that he wasn't even sure he could make the trek all the way back to the caves. But he knew he must try. Others were waiting, and someone else may have had better luck than him. At least he could get back much faster without needing to look in rooms and meander off into territory he had never been down before.

Opening the door to the steward's cabin, Finn was greeted with gasps, and Alma said, "Oh, my." Then everyone broke into cheers.

Finn looked around bewildered. "What?"

Russell tugged at the bottom of his sack. "Clearly you were the only one smart enough to gather clothing," he said with flushed cheeks.

"I feel like a new man," Finn boasted, smiling ear to ear. Still exhausted, however, he propped up against the door. "Any luck? Have Bill, Bertram, or June made it back?"

Alma was sitting on the bed with Monty's head in her lap as she gently snored. George sat at the opposite end near her feet. Russell was in the office chair, and he nodded. "Bill and Bertram have both been back and gone again, so far they found nothing, but each picked a room to go sleep in. I haven't seen June."

Finn was surprised to hear that, and even more surprised that George was still here and not off sleeping in one of the enormous anti-gravity beds that the rich had owned. "I noticed you said *they* found nothing." He raised his brow. Was he misinterpreting that, he wondered. "Does that mean…"

Russell nodded. His normal grim countenance opened to a grin, showing off the space between his front teeth. "I found a gap between the wall and a crack, similar to the one here." He pointed behind him. "It is wider, and I went in." He paused, licking his lips.

Finn leaned forward, his eyes flicking from Alma to Russell, waiting for the shoe to drop. "And?"

"It comes out in their home."

Finn released his breath. "Where was the breach? What did you see in there?"

"You know how the museum is laid out, where the crew area is visible?"

"Yes."

"I went in that direction, into the crew-members-only areas, where unless you took the tour at some point, passengers were not allowed. We had our own lounges and rec areas. There are some sleeping quarters for quick respites, and it was through one of those. I have to tell you, when I entered that wall, my heart never raced so fast in my life. I was terrified. What if I got to the end and they saw me? What would they do? And then you all would still be searching and maybe never find it again. Anyway, the crack is about twenty feet deep, and it brought me out to a tunnel, very much like the ones we live in down here. The only way I knew I was above our caves was the transparent floor, and a translucent ceiling. But some of the slugs were coming, and I didn't stick around to be caught. I came back here to wait for you guys."

"How did you hear them coming? Were they talking?"

Russell shook his head. "No, I heard no noise at all." He rubbed his fingers together and bowed his head, thinking. "It's more like a vibration, a push? I can't explain it, but I could feel them coming. You'll see."

"Okay, okay, this is all good. Now we get some rest and gather the troops to make an escape plan."

"I know you're exhausted, Finnegan, but you need to go out there and let the people know," Alma said.

Finn nodded. "Yeah, I know."

"I'll come with you," Russell offered.

"All right, I guess I'll see you in a few hours." He hated to go back to the nothing that was their lives for so many years, but he knew he couldn't talk to the people and then say goodnight and come back to a comfy bed. One more night of suffering, and they all could pick a bed of their choosing to rest in. He took the two steps across the floor and gave Alma a quick kiss on the forehead. "Goodnight."

~~~~~~

When Finnegan stepped out of the crevasse, the wall-to-wall mass of bodies went nuts. They stood, nudged the sleeping, and cheered loudly. At first, he was confused at the uproar. Russell elbowed him, and again he realized that he was the only person fully clothed. Paul wrapped his massive arms around Finn, slapping his back and fighting back tears of joy. He held him at arm's length. "It's true? This is really happening?"

First he looked up at the mass of slugs gathered above them. They were all crammed together, as his people were. Even his own Tattoo was there, and in that second, he wondered what they were thinking. The voices drew him back to the situation, and he addressed the people. "Yes." Finn grinned widely at the elation undulating through the crowded room. "Attention, everyone." He turned as he called out, and when the noise died down, he said, "Not only are most of the quarters intact…" He once again had to wait for the cheers to stop, but he never got the chance to finish speaking. As soon as people heard the ship was intact, they stopped listening.

The crowd rushed forward. The men weren't prepared for the reaction the news had aroused in people. Not hearing the pleas to wait, people began shoving into the crevasse.

"CALM DOWN! PEOPLE ARE GOING TO GET HURT!" Paul cried out but to no avail. All they could do was back away to safety and let the people push into the opening.

Finn could only imagine that on the other side of the wall, the ruckus would awaken Montana, as people began shooting out of the hole like candy from a Pez dispenser.

13. A New Day

After a restless sleep, Finnegan and Russell both promised Paul they would find a way in for him, as well as a few others who were too large-bodied to fit in the crack. Above them, the slugs continued to hover, either unaware that all the people were escaping, or unconcerned but the unusual happenings. Finn didn't care to wait around and found out. They slipped into the seemingly never-ending stream of people and shuffled back through to the ship.

"Thank goodness you are here," Alma said as soon as she saw their faces. "I swear I'm going to have permanent vertigo from the non-stop motion. The parade of people was bothersome, but I didn't want you guys to have to go off searching for us."

"Yeah, sorry about that. I had no idea this would happen," Finn said, sitting beside the girls.

"Can we go explore now?" Monty bounced on the mattress.

"Do you want to find your cabin, Alma? Perhaps get into some clothes again?" Finn asked.

Alma nodded. "Yes, I do, but what about gathering to make a plan for escape?"

"Everyone else disappeared anyway," Russell noted aloud. "We'll need to find men willing to enter the aliens' caves. Why don't we regroup in the captain's lounge in a few hours?"

"Ya, ya, let's go!" Monty pounced off the bed and pulled at Finn.

"All right, we can go to your room, Alma, and we'll see if we can find some clothes for Monty. Then we can see what the rest of humanity is up to," Finn agreed.

Alma stood, cracking her back, keeping out of the marching path of people. "I'm afraid to see what humanity is up to," she said as hooting and hollering echoed around the ship's corridors.

Finn shrugged. "It's better than moping about in dirt caves until we die." He lifted Monty into his arms as they cut into the exodus line and exited the small cabin.

Once they were out of the small room, the wide hallways of the ship allowed people to walk up to twenty abreast. It was less claustrophobic. The scene was worse than he feared. In the few hours he's been away, the people had already been ransacking the ship. It was as if they'd lost all control of their sensibility. There were clothes strewn from one end of the hall to the other. He wasn't sure why, unless people were just tearing into rooms and tossing what did not fit them.

Montana walked between Finn and Alma, her small hands clammy in each of theirs. Her eyes were as wide as saucers at everything to see. From the multi-patterned walls to the dome lights to the brightly colored fabrics of the clothes, her head rocketed left, right, up, down, and back again, trying to process it all.

As they passed the first cafeteria, a rank smell hit their nostrils through the open door.

"Ugh, what is that?" Monty asked. She had never smelt anything before other than perhaps stale breath.

Finn released Monty and took two steps into the room. There were thirty or forty people in the room, lying on the floor, sitting in the seats, or milling about. There was vomit and what appeared to be blood on the floor, tables, and seats. A few people were rolling on the floor, crying out and clutching their stomachs in pain. One man was even moaning, "Killmekillmekillmeoh," and Finn saw the open foil packages and foodstuffs tore open around them. He stepped back out and pressed the door closed, not wanting Monty to see the state the people were in.

"They tried to eat," he explained. "I am not sure what those pills do to us, but I do know they make our digestive system stop working. We'll get someone to come help them to the medical center."

Alma grimaced. "I bet they're in a lot of pain."

"From the sounds of it, yeah."

"Does that mean I won't get to try food?" Monty asked, and after the smell they just inhaled, Finn wasn't sure if she wanted to.

Finn rubbed her unruly curls. "Not to worry. We'll get it sorted out."

People danced, ran, laughed, and sang all around them as they made their way to Alma's old room. Finally reaching it, Finn stopped, recalling his emotions when he'd entered his own room, and said, "Go in, Alma. Reconnect and change, and then call us in. We'll just see if there is an empty room nearby to poke around in."

Alma pinched Finn's cheeks. "You're a good man, Finnegan." She patted the top of Monty's head. "Have fun." She opened her door, took a deep breath, and stepped in.

Finn turned Monty down the hall. A few rooms he tried were already locked, so they were occupied. One did open, and they went in. Monty hurried to the desk and pulled open the drawers. After finding a black, felt-tipped marker, she began to draw on the surface. Finn wasn't watching her, but opening the dresser to check out the clothes inside and see if anything would fit the child. He held up a pair of men's pants that would fit three of him in them, and he laughed. "Wrong room." He turned to show Monty and found her drawing on the table. He wanted to yell at her to stop but held back. It made no difference; there were no more rules to this life. "Come on, let's look some more. Bring the marker."

They checked three more rooms before he found some girl's clothes, and though they would still be too big for Monty, at least she could get dressed. He also found a Gaia emblazed notepad and brought that along. "Let's go wait for Alma, and she can help you dress."

Alma opened her door and waved Finn and Monty in. She was wearing a grey tweed jumpsuit, with hundreds of tiny mother-of-pearl buttons from her chin to her navel. Her hair was puffed up with a creamy chiffon wrap that held a prominent droopy bow on the left. She had even taken the time to add a peach blush to her cheeks and lips. On her feet were a pair of the fluffiest rabbit-fur slippers Finn had ever seen.

"You look ravishing!" Finn grinned and, not wanting to mess up her new outfit, blew her a kiss.

Monty stood with her mouth hanging open and then fell to her knees. At first, Finn gasped thinking the child had fainted, but then they burst into laughter when she pressed her cheeks into Alma's slippers.

"Come on, honey." Alma scooped the girl up. "Let's make you pretty too." She took the clothes out of Finn's arms and said, "Out."

A few long minutes later, the girls stepped back out into the hallway. Montana's smile split her face in two, and her cheeks were glowing. Alma had picked out a pair of soft turquoise leggings, that were all bunched up like errant leg warmers on her skinny legs. A thick set of mohair socks held them in place, and a mid-length pink sweater wrapped with a filigreed red belt kept the rest in order. Monty wriggled her bum, did a tiptoe jig, flapped her arms like a chicken, and hopped around the corridor.

"I think she likes it." Alma laughed.

"Great color scheme you have going on there."

"After endless shades of beige for seven years, I was ready to climb in that outfit myself."

Finnegan placed his arm over the older woman's shoulder. "I concur, but now I have work to do. I need to find the guys, and figure out how to get Paul in, and go find Helen."

"Of course, go." She shooed him, brushing him away with a double flick of her wrists. "I'll take Monty around and show her new wonders to keep her occupied. Please stay safe."

"I'll do my best," Finn said and turned to the child. He reached down, gathered her up in his arms, and planted a wet kiss on her cheek. "I have something I must do now. You stay with Alma, okay?"

Monty squirmed in his arms. Now that an entire new world opened up to her, she wanted to run and explore, to touch and smell and taste things. "Kay, see you later."

Alma held out her hand to the child. "Let's go explore."

As Finnegan trailed back to the crew area, he looked into the public shared areas. The first person he found was George Carlisle, Montana's dad, the last person he wanted to find.

"Hey, you all going to attack the slugs?" George called, running after Finn.

"We haven't discussed what we're doing."

"Well, I'm coming with."

"Why don't you stay here and enjoy your rebirth, George?"

"And miss all the fun?" George scoffed. "Not on your life."

Finn ignored the man and kept walking. They found Bertram attending to a rail of a man who had consumed candy bars. The man was covered in melted chocolate and dark brown streams of vomit. He was curled in the fetal position, and the doctor was rubbing his back and whispering in his ear.

"Hey, Doc?" Finn called, waving him away from the patient.

"What is it?"

"Can you come with us?"

The elderly doctor wrung his hands. "I think I am needed here now."

Finn shook his head. "Is there anything you can do for this?"

Bertram tapped the stethoscope around his neck, thinking. "Not in a medical sense, no. People have to understand our bodies do not work they way they used to. Perhaps if we stop taking the pills, our systems will reboot." His eyebrows furrowed. "But who's to say? We don't know what they were feeding us. This won't kill them though, they just need to relax and recover."

"We may actually need you, Doc," Finn pressed.

"All right, just give me a sec." Bertram spoke to the man on the floor and then proceeded with Finnegan and George.

They picked up Bill Davis, who still had not found Dartania, and the three continued to the crew area. As they passed one of the game rooms, Brenda Kelly came flying off a lounger and hollered for them to stop. With all heads turning to see what the shouting was about, they had no recourse but to wait for her to approach. She was dressed nurse-style, with black scrubs and a white cotton tee that revealed more than Finn wanted to see.

As she jogged toward them, her unfettered breasts bounced under her chin. "Sorry, fellas." She grinned, batting her eyes. "I just can't be restricted after all that time being practically nude."

"Can you keep it to a minimum please?" Finn asked, shifting his gaze around the crowded corridor.

"Touchy." She tried to lean her heavy breast against his arm and pretended not to notice when he took a step back. "Anyway, what can I do to help?"

"You can piss off," George growled, and Brenda stuck out her tongue at him.

Bertram tsked and folded his arms.

"You can do me a huge favor," Finn said, leaning closer to her. That quieted her down. "Can you find the largest men's clothes you are able and take them to Paul? I don't feel right leaving him down there and at least not tossing him some comfort."

Brenda winked. "Anything for you, Finnegan." She turned and headed off.

"Let's hurry before we find another tagalong," Bertram said.

The guys made the rest of the way to the crew area without being accosted. They found Preston and Russell waiting for them. The men stood from the benches they were lying on.

"Took you long enough," Preston said.

Russell looked at the group. "This is our entry team?"

"Unless you have a better plan. Paul is trapped in the tunnels still, and these guys were with us from the beginning," Finn said.

"Yeah, what's wrong with us?" George huffed.

"How the hell would I know? I'm no psychiatrist," Russell countered.

Finn held up his hands. "Look, I know this isn't the best fighting team, but we don't even know what we're going to encounter in there. We can't put out a casting call for strong, able-bodied men to make a team—"

"But the humble will inherit the land and will delight themselves in abundant prosperity." A soft voice broke Finn's words, and they turned to find Pastor Mayweather walking toward them.

"Ah, Jesus," Finn uttered.

Mayweather continued. "Some boast in chariots and some in horses, but we will boast in the name of the Lord our God. They have bowed down and fallen, but we have risen and stood upright." He stopped before Finnegan, commanded his attention with just a gaze, and finished. "Behold, I am going to send an angel before you to guard you along the way and to bring you into the place which I have prepared. Be on your guard before him and obey his voice; do not be rebellious toward him, for he will not pardon your transgression since my name is in him. But if you truly obey his voice and do all that I say, then I will be an enemy to your enemies and an adversary to your adversaries."

"What does any of this shit even mean?" Finnegan asked.

"Finnegan Brennan, listen to your heart," Mayweather said as he turned and walked away.

"What an odd fellow." Finn shook it off, having no time for the pastor's shenanigans.

Bill crossed his arms. "I don't know, guys. I think he's warning us."

Finn had enough of the pastor and his so-called prophecy. "Let's find some weapons and get in there."

"Here." Preston went to the bench and lifted off supplies for the men. Because they never had weapons of any kind on the ship, the two previous crew members had found tools that could be of assistance. Finnegan was handed a four-inch-thick crowbar. Bill, an almost ten-pound wrench. George, a three-foot-long socket wrench. Preston and Russell each had steel bars, whose everyday purpose wasn't clear.

"I think, for the time being, we need to sneak in, assess the situation, get a lay of the land, get out, and then talk strategy," Russell said.

"We have no idea what we're in for," Bill added. "So yeah, whatever works."

The other men nodded, nerves putting them on edge and causing their palms to sweat. They all needed to get moving.

"Take us there." Finn nodded.

Russell took the group to crack in the ship. Once again, it opened to a fissure in the wall, only this time, to the upper portion where the aliens lived.

Weapons held at ready, they slipped one by one out of the wall and into the slugs' domain. Finn marveled at the transparent floor beneath his feet. He could see the tunnels below as clear as day, and it was a surreal experience to be topside of that view after all those years of looking up. It was exactly as he had imagined it only days before. Naturally, they looked up and were shocked. The ceiling, forty feet above, was translucent, similar to the floor beneath their feet.

"Is that the sky?" Bill asked.

"Holy shit! It must be," Preston said.

"Ah that's why it's always light." Finn looked down. "Two suns on Kepler—no night, no solid roof…and no solid floor."

"It's foggy, though, I can't see the sky," George said.

"Hey, it's the first outside we've seen in seven years, why don't you just enjoy the moment?" Russell glared at George.

"Psst." Preston caught everyone's attention. "We don't want to get lost in here. Should someone stay here to call out the location if needed?"

George nodded. "Ya, good idea. I'll stay here."

Finn rolled his eyes. "Of course you will. I'm going this way. The rest of you do what you want." Staying close to the wall, he moved right, trying to picture where above their colony they were positioned at the moment.

As he crept down the corridor, he looked into empty chambers that were almost identical to their own sleeping areas. The only change was the slugs did not have platforms to lay upon. This made him wonder if the slugs didn't just follow them randomly but followed whoever ended sleeping below them. *No wonder they were always there even when we slept.* He pondered this new thought as he moved quietly past empty room after empty room. *Where are they? We're here, and they always follow us.* He recalled that Alma told him the slug would stay at the entrance to the crevasse whenever Dartania disappeared. *What, all the slugs are still back in that one area?* He questioned himself, without answers, as he walked on.

Eventually, the floor began to slope upward and gradually changed from transparent to opaque to solid, and once again, he was on rock ground. The tunnel opened to a spacious chamber, more significant than any they had below, with multiple offshoots. It was eerily silent here, and Finn paused before deciding to continue straight through.

The chambers here were different. Each new room he passed had things in them, alien objects that he could not identify nor understand. He supposed this was where they lived, and the other chambers were just where they slept, if they slept. As he approached another larger opening ahead, he felt a strange vibration. It began low, almost like a tickle on the front of his body. As he moved forward, it became stronger. He could feel it humming through him. His bladder, kidneys, heart, everything rattled inside his body. Still, he pressed forward. Then it began to affect him. It pressed him back, his teeth chattered, and the crowbar in his hand bounced with the push. Ten feet from the opening, he could see them. The slugs were crammed together, hundreds of them, and although he had moved upward in the tunnels, he deduced they were all above the women's area. They were waiting for the humans to return from the unseen place in the wall. Now that he was within closer proximity to them, he realized they did not resemble slugs at all. They were about fourteen feet tall, with conical shaped bodies. They appeared more worm-like, with hundreds of fine rings segmenting their bodies. He couldn't tell if they had heads, or faces, but he wasn't about to find out.

He stepped back slowly, hoping to not draw any attention. With each step farther, the vibrations lessened. The crowbar stopped dancing, and his teeth stopped chattering. The tickle came and went. He turned and ran back, straight through, past the empty rooms to where George was pacing at the crack in the wall.

"Did you find anything?"

"Just them. A lot of them."

"Nothing else? No escape hatch, no stairs out, no spaceship?"

Finnegan narrowed his eyes at the man and shook his head. "I'm going this way now to find the others."

"Fine, yup, I'll just wait here." George waved him off.

Ignoring the small man, Finn went left after the other men. Again, he passed empty chambers and various offshoots. Reaching a large opening that had multiple similar tunnels, Finn kept left this time. The ground sloped upward, but this time there were no vibrations. As he neared the end, he did pick up low voices. He crouched low against the wall, moving cautiously toward an opening. Nearing a large cavern, he spotted the backside of Bill.

Finn stood erect and stepped through the entrance. He soon stopped dead in his tracks. Unaware of what he was doing, he ran forward. The men spotted him and moved aside. Finn walked up to the clear wall and pressed his palm up against it. "Helen?" he called.

"We've tried, Finn. Either they can't hear us or they're doped up," Preston told him.

On the opposite side of the wall was the botanical garden from Gaia, along with two of the botanists that had worked it. Helen just happened to be near the wall, collecting samples. The men said they had been pounding on it and yelling at her for a while, and she never even turned to look.

"Well, let's go through these tunnels and find a way in." Finn pushed to move past the others when he felt the vibrations again. "They're coming."

"What? Who?" Bill spun as if someone was creeping up on them. He felt the wrench softly vibrating in his hand. "What is that?"

"I encountered hundreds of the slugs back that way, and this is what I felt before I saw them. Only it was a lot worse."

"Ugh, it makes my stomach ache." Preston grimaced.

"Ya, we'd better…" Finn was about to say, "get out of here," when one of the slugs came out of one of the tunnels and into the chamber with them.

Now that they all saw one up close, they, too, noticed it didn't look much like a slug. It stood—if you could call it standing, without legs—six to eight feet above the men. It was a rusty brown and had no discernible eyes, ears, or mouth.

Seeing or sensing the men, it became rigid and then straightened itself taller, and began to undulate in a weird pulsating movement from the ground up. The vibration gave off a low keening noise that hurt the men's eardrums.

They all cried out and covered their ears.

Russell screamed and bolted forward, the pipe extended in his fists. He jabbed it directly into the creature's lower body.

As the pipe pierced its thick outer layer, two things happened simultaneously. A woman screamed, "NOOOOOO!" and the alien deflated into a dry heap, while the vibration changed from a hum to an outright sonic boom.

The humans in the room were knocked flat on their backs. The air whooshed out of the tunnels and then back in again with a deafening roar.

A few seconds later, Finn sat up shaking his head. He looked around and saw Dartania sprawled out a few feet away from the dead alien. "Dartania?" He rushed over to her as the others gathered themselves.

Her eyes opened, blinking. Then they widened, and she pushed Finnegan away. "What did you do?" She crawled to the carcass.

"I was protecting us." Russell didn't try to pull the pipe from under the body of the slug. He poked at it with his toe. "Why are you here? What's going on?"

Tears ran down her cheeks as she went to pet the dead thing, then must've thought better of it and pulled back. "They don't hurt us." Her eyes flicked from Finn to the others. "They saved us, and you." She stood quickly, her fists clenched, white-knuckled, and got into Russell's face. "You killed them. That's what wrong with MEN! YOU KILL!" she shrieked.

They all froze as the air around them began to vibrate again. They could feel it tickle the bottoms of their feet. Even now with shoes on, it moved up their legs and into their spines.

"They're coming," Finn said, and no one moved.

"What do we do, Dartania?" Bill asked.

"Get rid of those tools and sit." She sat on the hard ground in front of them with her legs crossed. She was the only one still in the sack dress.

Not sure if they should believe the young woman or not, the men looked about wildly. Finnegan sat first and placed his crowbar on the ground behind him, so if things went wrong, it was within reach. The others followed suit.

As the group of aliens appeared at the mouth of the tunnel, the vibrations grew to the point where the men's teeth were chattering.

"Uuuhhh, wwwwhaattt'ss gonnna haaappppenn?" Preston said.

No one replied.

Dartania raised her arms straight out from the sides of her body and began to wave them up and down in opposing directions. It looked as if she was trying to fly.

The creatures had stopped before the large central opening, and the one who appeared to be in charge was a few feet closer. It bolted straight up, similar to what the one they'd killed had done, then it wriggled side to side.

Dartania waved her arms forward and backward now.

The creature wriggled up and down.

Dartania moved her arms to the front and again waved them up and down in opposing fashion.

The creature flopped onto its side and began slithering in a circle.

That's when Finnegan saw the blue anchor on its underside. He leaned forward, whispering, "That's Tattoo. Are you talking to them?"

"Shh," she said, still moving her arms in various and seemingly odd positions.

Tattoo returned to an upright stance and remained perfectly still. The group of aliens behind it all turned as one and retreated through the passageway. The tickling sensations went with them.

"Thank God. That was driving me nuts." Russell shook his head to rid himself of the feeling.

Dartania turned to the men and said, "They are trusting us. Come on."

"Trusting us?"

"How can you talk to them? How do you know all this?"

"What the hell is going on here?"

The questions flew at the girl, and Finnegan stood. "Calm down. We don't want her running off again. In some crazy way, she knows how to communicate with them. Let's just start with that and follow her."

Russell grabbed Finn's arm. "What if she has no clue and we're being led into a trap?"

"What difference does it make, Russ? Clearly, we aren't leaving anyway." Finn spun in a half circle. "Do you see computers? Equipment? Electronics of any kind? These things, slugs, Keplerworms, whatever they are, are not of a technological society."

"He's not wrong." Preston shrugged, and they all followed Dartania and the worms.

14. A New Life

Bill pushed past the others to be closer to Dartania. "Can you tell us how you can understand these things?"

Dartania turned slightly to eye her uncle. She must have decided he only had good intentions and said, "I hear their meaning in the vibrations. There are no words here. I answer them with my own vibrations."

"Ah, the air displacement from her arms." Preston nodded, understanding the basic principle.

"Nuts regardless," Bill whispered over his shoulder, and Dartania lifted a lip in his direction.

The ground beneath their feet sloped ever upward, and the climb was becoming sharper. Finn could feel the strain of unused muscles.

"Where are we going?" Finnegan asked.

"Up," Dartania replied.

"No shit, ya think?" Preston said.

They kept climbing. The tunnel that was two-abreast wide continued to widen farther until it leveled out. At the end of the long hall, they found themselves on a vast flat plain, covered by another transparent ceiling. There was nothing but hard rock as far as the eye could see. The sky above always lit with two suns was hazy. There was no blue hue like on Earth, no discernible moons, no fluffy white clouds painting animals in the sky.

It hit Finnegan at that moment that Earth was gone; home was gone. Though they knew it for years and had lived trapped for seven of them, seeing an alien sky from the ground for the first time broke his heart. Silent tears fell from his eyes as he stared upward.

The Keplerworm turned, it's body undulated, and Dartania translated for them. "The air outside of the tunnels is what knocks us out. They saved us—are saving us."

Russell took two fast steps toward the alien. Feeling threatened, it pushed its upper body outward, creating a flash of vibration so intense, it knocked Russell to his ass with an *oomph*. "Hey!" he cried out.

Dartania sidestepped to block Russell's view of the being. "Don't do that again."

He held up his hands. "All right. I only wanted to know why, if they are saving us, did they lock us underground with nothing? Ask it that why don't you?"

"No," she replied.

"No? What do you mean no?" He stood and brushed off his rear.

Finnegan stepped in. He'd been watching the creature and thinking about the big picture. "I think I get it," he said. "Just like with the technology, they don't have possessions. They don't wear clothes. They don't have hands, or eyes, or ears. They just live. I think that is what they gave us too. A place to be alive."

Dartania nodded. "Yes." Her long ebony hair folded across her face as she bowed her head to Finn.

"But what about Helen and the others?" Finn asked. "What do they do to them? Why do they have them here?"

Dartania turned and waved her arms about. She paused while the creature wiggled and wove, and then she made more of her own motions. Turning back to face the men, she said, "Well, we aren't talking in words here. Best I can tell you is that they keep the plants alive to feed us. They create water from the ship, the air, and the plants, to help the plants-huh-I don't understand." She shook it off and kept talking. "They need the knowledgeable ones to help. It makes us, well those people in there, happy too." She turned to Finn. "Helen has been here before and always returned better, right?"

"Well, the one time I knew she went away and came back, yes."

"You mean those pills we eat every day are from our own plants?" Preston blinked in surprise. "But how? I could eat salad for days on Earth and still be hungry and poop! Why don't we poop?"

Dartania's stoic expression broke at this point. Her head tilted back, and she began to laugh.

Bill's eyebrow went up. "What's so funny?"

"You explain excrement to a being that has never done that in its lifetime." Her light brown eyes sparkled with the moment, and for the first time since meeting her, Finnegan felt affection for the young woman who was opening up the lines of communication for them.

"You know what?"

All eyes turned toward Finn.

"I think we are going to have a lot of time to learn about how this all works. It's been really long few days. Can we rest and talk later?" His eyes flicked to the Keplerworm. He felt it understood what he said, as it wriggled only the tip of its bottom end where the tattoo was.

Though they had too many questions on their minds, they followed the alien back to the large cavern where they met. Finn walked over to the clear wall where he had seen Helen. She was no longer there. He planted his forehead on the surface…then his palm. Without turning, he said, "She will be back, right?"

"Yes," Dartania soon replied, and Finn could only assume that she'd asked the question and received an answer on his behalf.

"I'm sorry about…" Russell pointed at the dried-up pile of flesh that was once a living being. He'd never killed anything before.

They moved together back through the tunnels to the fissure in the wall. Tattoo did not follow.

Without any resistance, or seeing more aliens, they slipped back into Gaia. George was standing on the outside of the door to the room, holding his pipe in both hands. "What took you so long? What happened? Did you see the aliens? I tried to warn you, but—"

"Yes, I see how you tried to warn us," Finnegan said, cutting him off. He pushed past the beady-eyed man and proceeded to his room.

"We are fine, George, but we have lots to talk about tomorrow," Preston said, filling the man in that much.

It made no difference. George disappeared back into his own world and never returned to the group efforts again.

~~~~~~

The chair creaked, old wood on old wood, a meditative sound lulling Finn into his peaceful state before sleep. The stars winked on one by one as twilight descended over the land. The mountains became looming deep shadows, blanketing the creatures within, so they could awaken and live in the silence of night. He inhaled the scent of pine, sweet summer grass, and the evaporating lake in the air. From deep in the woods, a pack of wolves began their howling night calls, and an owl hooted in reply. Closing his eyes, Finn embraced the simple life he had built for himself, knowing that one day in the future, all of this would be no more. He pushed that thought away, there was no better life than earth, and he would savor every scent, sound, taste, and sight. Darkness began to fold him away to sleep...

His eyes opened, and for one fleeting moment, he could smell the forest, and then he blinked. The vision before him caused confusion; he was looking at the simple desk in his room on Gaia. He blinked again, and the day before came flooding back. It wasn't another dream. They were on the ship. They broke in, or broke out, depending on your standpoint. They saw the aliens, they killed an alien. They were free and yet not free. He sat up. "Time to start over," he said to the room and pulled on fresh clothes.

    Finnegan went straight to Alma's room. As he walked through the corridors, he watched the people running, laughing, talking, and acting more human than they had in years. A few who had heard the pastor's sermons slapped him on the back or shook his hand, thanking him for saving them. He knew full well it was Dartania who'd saved them, and he would have to figure out how to rectify that fact. He didn't want the attention or their praise. Arriving at Alma's, he knocked, and the door whisked quickly open.

    Alma appeared a finger to her lips. Finn peeked around her and saw Montana curled in the bed. Her cheeks had a rosy glow that he'd never seen on her before. Her small hands were tucked under her chin, and a smile frozen on her lips. Alma nudged him back out the door. "Come see," she said.

    She led Finn to one of the movie theaters on the same level. It was filled wall to wall with people talking and staring in awe at the once-white wall where a movie would play. Now, that wall was covered floor to ceiling in a mural so lifelike, Finn felt he could step across the border and be inside that place. His eyes roved across the landscape before him. There were low lands of windswept teal grass, with azure cumulus clouds against a blazing white sun. Jagged-edged black mountains soared into the skyline, and strange, three-legged beasts feasted on coral-spiked bushes. Along the left side of the mural, squat round huts were built on black shimmering ground, and humans milled about in various acts of living. One older woman with grey waves of hair was hanging laundry on a line strung between two huts.

Alma took Finn's hand and pulled him through the crowd.

"Why are you showing me this?" he asked. Then it hit him. "Did Monty do this? No." He shook his head. "That's not possible."

"Look." Now that they were closer to the wall, she pointed up at the people. "Look at it, Finnegan."

He squinted, reaching out to touch the faces in the village, gasped, and drew back. "Is that us?"

Alma's white teeth gleamed as her smile grew. "That's me." She pointed to the woman hanging the laundry. "And that's you." She couldn't reach, but her finger aimed up higher.

He tilted his head back and looked up. In the center of the houses was a woman sitting in a rocking chair, holding a baby out as a man reached down to take it. Finn looked about wildly, spotted the ladder that would have been required to paint such a mural, and pushed through the people to grab it. He rushed up a few rungs to get closer to the painting. This time, he did touch it. It was Helen holding a baby, and none other than himself leaning down, arms out to receive. "It is us!"

Alma laughed. "Isn't it wonderful?"

"And Monty did this all by herself? Last night?"

"Yes, we found some art supplies, and she became a child possessed. I'm telling you, Finn, it was a sight to behold. You can ask anyone here." The crowd nodded in agreement, voices murmuring at the miracle they witnessed.

"No wonder she's so tired. Granted, it's as good as the Sistine Chapel, who knew we had Michelangelo in our midst? But what's all the hoopla about?" He indicated the room full of quiet people.

"They believe it's not just a painting but a prophecy, a vision of our future."

"Ah, not more of this crap. Is Mayweather involved?"

"No, I haven't seen him." Alma kept her eyes on the painting. "How do you explain the scene though? This is a child that has only been subject to the art in the gallery her entire life. This…" She inhaled sharply. "This is visionary."

Finnegan took Alma by the arm and led her out of the room. "Sure, but isn't all art visionary? I mean, did Picasso draw people all mixed up because that's how he saw them? It's just art, Alma."

"Perhaps, but anyways, tell me about your trip to the aliens. What happened?"

Finn filled her in on everything that transpired and how it looked as though there was no way off the planet, therefore bringing her up to speed on why he thought Monty was not a prophet of any sorts.

"Dartania can speak to them? Interesting. What do we do now?"

"We need to make all the people aware that the slugs, uh, worms, are not out to hurt us and try to talk to them about who we are and what we really need to survive."

"And see if we can enlist their help to get Paul and the others who could not fit through the hole into the ship," Alma pointed out.

"Oh, shit. I completely forgot about them. I guess we'd better get to that first."

At that precise moment, Pastor Mayweather approached from the other direction and said, "Do not withhold good from those to whom it is due when it is in your power to act."

Finn held up his hand. "Can you just talk like a person for once?"

"My apologies, Finnegan. It helps me to remember Bible passages by speaking them in useful situations. No harm meant. Why don't you see if the microphones still work? You can speak to the entire human race in one fell." Mayweather gave a tiny smile, dipped his head, and continued on his way.

"That's a great idea. Do you mind staying with Montana? I'll come back later."

"Not at all, Finn. You go do what needs doing. We'll be here." Alma returned to her room and Monty.

Finn worked his way back to the crew area. He checked the doors until he found the one labeled Captain Emerson and knocked. After a brief wait, Russell's door opened, and he stood in a pair of briefs, rubbing his eyes. "Finn, what's up?"

"Can you come with me to the main cockpit and see if we can get the announcement systems to work?"

Russell perked up instantly. "Yes, we haven't checked out any of the systems yet." He threw on some clothes, and they headed off.

They talked future as they walked, and Finn told him about the mural that Russell must make a point to see, and how they needed to tell the people that the aliens are harmless. As they left the sleeping quarters, they were met by a solid rock wall.

Finn slapped it. "The museum," he said.

Russell nodded. "I hadn't thought of that. The front of the ship is underground. Damn it!" He tapped his temple, thinking. "There are communication outposts in various positions so the crew could speak to the cabin if needed. Do you think if I take you there you can wire it up to cover the ship?"

Finnegan shrugged. "I would have to see it to know."

"Come this way then." Russell turned back and then took a corridor left. They wove through the rooms until he opened a hidden panel on the ship's inside wall.

"Hey, I never knew these were here," Finn said, touching the invisible switch.

"That's the point. Only the captains and stewards knew. Here." He opened a smaller compartment in the cubby, and a control panel with a tiny earbud popped out.

Finnegan checked the small system. He figured if most of the emergency lights, the doors, and other random things still worked on the ship, then this should work too. He lifted the casing and began to move wires from one conductor to another. After a few minutes, he tapped the earbud and sure enough, the sound echoed from the speakers in the ceiling. "Ha it worked!"

Russell slapped his back. "Good job. Now what are you going to say?"

"I…uh…" Finn stammered. "I didn't think about that."

"Okay, I'm one of the captains of this ship. I should do it anyway. Give it here."

Finn gladly handed over the earbud. The last thing he wanted was for Mayweather to say, "See, you are the leader."

Russell cleared his throat, placed the bud in his ear, and spoke.

"Attention, everyone. Attention. Attention. This is Captain Emerson speaking. Please listen carefully. We have reached the aliens and ascertained that they did not intend to harm us. I repeat, they are friendly. They are simple creatures that have no understanding of humans' way of life. We will need to work with them to gain understanding of them, and they of us. Please have patience a little longer. Enjoy your rooms and the simple pleasures we have back. We will keep you all posted of any possible exodus. The important thing is not to harm the aliens if you see them. They will not harm us."

As he was about to sign off, Finn whispered, "Tell them not to eat."

"Huh?" Russell leaned in. "What do you mean?"

"I saw people deathly ill that attempted to eat food again. Just tell them not to do it."

Russell tapped the bud. "Whatever you do, don't eat food. Do not attempt to eat food." Finn gave him a thumbs-up, and Russell finished, saying, "We will post updates as they arrive. Everyone enjoy the luxuries and relax."

"Oh, and ask…" Finn began, and Russell handed him the earpiece.

"You ask."

Finn took it, placed the warm jellybean-shaped node in his ear, and spoke. "Dartania Aswar, please meet us in the crew lounge."

Russell raised his brow.

"We need to enlist the aliens help to get Paul and the others out of the tunnels.

Finn and Russell worked their way back toward the lounge. Upon arrival, they found Alma, Montana, Brenda, and Dartania all there waiting. Montana jumped into Finnegan's arms and planted wet kisses on his cheeks.

"Hey, kiddo! How you doing? You look great." He praised her new outfit that consisted of a long-sleeved purple shirt, covered with a short-sleeved orange shirt, grey leopard leggings, a plaid skirt, and ruby-red shoes.

"Did you see my picture?" She grinned and squirmed to be put down.

"Yes, it's amazing. You are a talented lady. You know that?"

Monty shrugged. "I saw that place in my dreams. Someday we'll all live there."

Finn ruffled her hair but said nothing to her. He addressed Alma, eyebrows raised. "What's up?"

"She can meet them." Alma surely understood the implications. "It will happen sooner or later, why not now?"

"I want to help too." Brenda stepped in closer to Finnegan, attempting to brush against him.

He shuffled away so she wouldn't. "Well, we don't need an entourage. We just need to see if Dartania here can get them to help Paul and the others left behind."

Dartania nodded and turned without speaking to head through the crack again.

Everyone followed her. Finn kept Monty between himself and Alma. Dartania led them back to the large cavern where the walled-off plants were. Montana rushed forward, having never gotten to see living plants in her life. She pressed her nose up against the transparent rock. "Can I go in there?"

No one had time to respond when the vibrations began to tickle their skin. Three Keplerworms entered the chamber, and Dartania began her wigging-arms speaking. Monty turned and watched, transfixed by the beings. She grinned and waved hello, and one of the three identical aliens waggled the tip of its body, making her laugh.

"Hey, Dartania, ask if I can go in the…uh, plants?" Montana said, forgetting the correct terminology.

"I don't think that's a good idea," Finn responded quickly, remembering the flesh-eating plants and poisonous ones that without a proper guide could kill the child.

Monty was about to protest when Dartania said, "They say wait. Later."

While Finn was relieved, the child pouted, and then Dartania said, "Follow them."

The group followed the vibrating worms through the tunnel system that was their home. Whenever they passed larger groups of the creatures, the vibrations would intensify to almost painful proportions and then reside as they moved on.

Finnegan began to think that was why they did not attempt to interact with the humans all this time; they knew the sentient creatures would not be able to handle the constant vibration. Montana, meanwhile, marveled and chattered at the clear floor beneath their feet, pointing out various people's pods, including hers, Helen's, Alma's and Finn's. She knew exactly where they were.

Finally, they reached the women's area, and the worms stopped. They danced about, and Dartania translated. "We wait here while they dig."

They watched in fascination as the three creatures wound themselves together into one fat worm with three heads and three tails. Alma wrapped her arms around Monty and sat against the tunnel wall as the fat worm entered a chamber across from them. It moved to the wall and pressed itself against the solid rock. The vibrations emanated from them, causing the tunnels surrounding everyone to hum. They could feel it in their feet and against the rock. The worms acted as a horizontal jackhammer, and dirt began to fall away as a tunnel opened before them. They pressed forward, sinking deeper and deeper into the wall. Then they disappeared from the humans' sight.

Finnegan, Russell, Brenda, Dartania, Alma, and Montana all watched in awe as before long, the unified Keplerworm appeared in the cavern below them. Together, the three had bore a hole through the side of impenetrable rock, turned downward, and came out in an entirely new spot.

"Wow…just…wow," Russell stammered.

"So that is how all this was made." Brenda whistled.

"Okay, guys. We'd better get down there before one of the people see the aliens and freak out," Finn said and entered the newly formed tunnel that was wide enough for two humans to walk side by side.

They were even more surprised to find that the tunnel did a twist and gave them a gentle slope downward, and they eased out back into their unwanted home. As soon as they got out, the worms unwound themselves, and each returned to the tunnel and their own home.

"Paul? Hello? Anyone?" Brenda shouted and looked up and down the tunnel. They were only one chamber over from the fissure, but from above, they had not seen any people.

A voice yelled back, "Hello? Who's there?"

"Paul, it's us. Uh, Finnegan and the others," Brenda shouted back.

Paul's head poked out of one of the rooms. "HEY!" he boomed. "How'd you get here? Everyone," he shouted loudly. "We're saved."

Other people came cautiously out of the sleeping pods and, seeing the group, cheered and rushed over.

June was among them. "I came back to show them they weren't abandoned," she said to the rescue team.

"Very kind of you." Finnegan nodded at her.

Russell gave them a brief overview of what they'd found, how the aliens worked, and that so far they were still trapped, but that life would be a bit easier now. Together, they all returned to the upper tunnels.

~~~~~

As the next day approached, the people realized they still needed their life-sustaining pills. They couldn't eat human food, and the pills had always been left for them in the tunnels. A group traveled back down and gathered as many of the pills as they could to share. Finnegan once again went with Dartania to talk to the Keplerworms, and Monty tagged along.

"Can you teach us how to talk to them too?" he asked her.

"I do it. I can't explain it," she said under her breath.

"Okay, I'll watch you, and you tell me what you are saying to them when you wave your arms like you do."

Dartania simply nodded. She led them back to the same place as always, and they waited. Montana saw Helen through the clear rock wall and went running over. She pounded on the wall, yelling for her attention, but once again, Helen did not respond. When the Keplerworm appeared, Monty turned, tears streaming down her face, and screamed, "Let her out! Give me back my mom!"

"Whoa." Finnegan ran to her side and held her from flinging herself at the alien.

It waved frantically, and Dartania translated. "The sky is open in the room. The air makes us odd. They can return later."

Finnegan looked at the sky and realized that it wasn't fog at all. The very air of the planet was a gaseous liquid. "That is what they used to knock us out all the time. They must have holes they can open and close to control the volume of air let in. Sometimes it knocks us out. Other times, it merely leaves us in this zombie state that Helen is in now. Dartania, can you tell them how important she is to us and that we need her now?"

"I'll try." Dartania flapped her arms, wiggled them, wound them together, and waved.

Finnegan understood not one sign of it.

"Okay, cover your mouths," she said and pulled the neck of her shirt up over her face.

With a rumble, the clear wall began to slide on an invisible track. It opened three feet and stopped, tendrils of the heavy air wisped out the opening, and suddenly Helen was floating. Finnegan looked from the worm to Helen, down to Monty, and back again. He watched Helen glide, now horizontal on her back—slowly and without a fight, a foot off the ground—out through the large opening and then set gently near them. The clear wall slid soundlessly closed, and the air cleared.

Monty ran and knelt at Helen's side.

Finnegan did the same and took her hand. "Helen?"

Her eyes fluttered open. "Finn?" She smiled then spotted Montana. "Monty? What's going on?" She pulled herself up, and Monty climbed into her lap. Helen automatically stroked the child's hair. Then her eyes widened. She looked Finn up and down, and held Monty at arm's length. Her eyes flicked between the two, and then she spotted the garden. "What! You have clothes? The garden?" Her head spun, and she saw the worm for the first time, a scream clearly building in her chest.

"Wait!" Finn pinched her chin in his fingers. "Helen look at me." Her eyes focused on him. "It's okay. We are safe. You are safe. We found Gaia, and we can talk to the aliens—well, she can." He waved at Dartania. "We have a lot to tell you."

Montana climbed off her lap as Finnegan helped Helen stand. "Let's get you comfortable, and we'll tell you everything." He looped his arm through hers, Monty took her free hand, and they headed back toward the ship. Over his shoulder, Finnegan called to Dartania, "Tell them we need the pills delivered to the ship from now on. We'll be back to talk."

15. A Life Lived

We were free yet not free. We were kept.

As time went on, many of us learned how to talk in waves to the Keplerworms. The aliens did not see or hear as we did. The best we could understand was that they picked up sonic waves much like the earth bat. We discovered the reason they gassed us when we acted up was for our own protection. Those who had attempted suicide were still alive. One time, they showed us a chamber filled with our people who were asleep. They allowed a specific amount of the air into the chamber, and it kept them sleeping. How they could know the exact amount, or that it wouldn't harm the humans, we could not understand. One by one, we had them awakened and returned to Gaia with us, where they would be happier than in the tunnels.

We learned the creatures fed us by way of our own botanical garden and a mix of the elements the worms consumed from within the planet. Our scientists worked on studying the composite material to try to discover how it stopped us from defecating and why we no longer required water. So far, no big breakthroughs, but it keeps them busy.

Everyone was more content to be with their belongings again, to have beds, blankets, and darkness when they wanted. But the pills still took away our human desires, and there were no new children being created.

Bertram Grant still played doctor. Even though no one ever got sick, it gave him a purpose and people humored him. Bill Davis and Brenda Kelly took a liking to each other. I was thankful for that. The last thing I needed was her constantly hanging off of me. Dartania continued to keep to her own little world. She enjoyed talking to Monty and the aliens, who she seemed to understand easier than humans. Alma helped many people through tough mental times. She still monitored Montana, but Helen and I did not see Alma as much. Pastor Carl Mayweather continued to hold his "predictive" services, which had high attendance. I was not one of them. I still found it laughable that his previous predictions were all wrong, but no one else seemed to care.

We knew this life under Kepler, in Gaia, was still not enough. Russell, Paul, Preston, and I worked closely with other engineers and computer programmers until we were able to get Gaia's systems back to power. With the ship cleaved in two, there was no way for us to get off the planet. We were successful in reactivating the communications and turned on the distress signal. We took turns manning the center and not only reached out to other ships and planets but listened for signs of life as well. Two years passed living on Gaia and nothing, but we have not given up hope.

As Montana grew older, her dreams never stopped. She drew almost daily. Her mural that began in the movie theater, rounded the corner into the hallways. It stretched for miles throughout Gaia. She was showing us the new planet where we would one day reside, and she would be blessed with a little sister…or so she liked to tell us. Helen and I were now Mom and Dad to her. George was barely ever seen. No one knew what he was doing, and no one cared. One day, she had the Keplerworms open a fissure into the art gallery, and now her room was filled with her favorite paintings. The Chameleon hung over her bed as she'd always wished.

Perhaps her dreams are real.

Helen and the other botanists learned of how they worked by rote in the gaseous garden and, now armed with respirators, were able to come and go as they pleased. The Keplerworms could never enter the space because their vibrations tended to kill the plants, but they always stayed and watched. They, too, enjoyed the greenery, the blooming flowers, and vibrations the plants gave off. They told us it was soothing, quieter than us. I believed them. Of course, no one could predict if Gaia's systems would ever stop working, for if that day came, there would be no artificial light or a way to generate water to feed the plants. That would be disastrous for all.

Tattoo and I spent more time together wandering the tunnels. It was hard to talk to them while moving, but we were just used to each other I suppose.

While this was not the life I expected to end up with, it was the life I learned to live. As long as we had each other, and no more fear of being gassed, we were happy.

Loving each other is really all we needed anyway.

The words of Finnegan Brennan, 3023 (or thereabout), from Gaia, kept on Kepler.

The End

I HOPE YOU ENJOYED THIS FORAY INTO A NEW WORLD. PLEASE DON'T FORGET TO LEAVE A REVIEW.

YOU ARE WELCOME TO CONTACT ME PERSONALLY THROUGH MY WEBSITE HTTP://THERESAJCBS.WIXSITE.COM/AUTHORPAGE

WHERE YOU CAN EMAIL, SIGN UP FOR NEWS, OR FIND MY FACEBOOK AND TWITTER PAGES.

I LOOK FORWARD TO DISCUSSING THIS BOOK, OR ANY OTHERS WITH YOU.

SINCERELY THERESA JACOBS

Made in the USA
Columbia, SC
10 August 2018